MW01124570

Copyright 2015 by Josi Beck
PROJECT: Killer

Cover Design By Louisa Maggio at LM CREATIONS

Editing & Formatting by
Rogena Mitchell Jones Manuscript Service
Proofread by Ami Hadley of RMJ Manuscript Service

contents for project: k'ller
— if you dare.

dedication

To my entire support team, beta team, and fans—writing books wouldn't be possible without you.

prologue

KILLER

IT ALL STARTED with a *kiss*.

It wasn't one of those sappy ass ones, either. You know, where there is affection with electricity flowing through your body and you just fucking know they're the one for you. No, this was a different kind of kiss. It wasn't a spark, but a mere touch of one's skin against another. I would like to think that somehow the simple gesture had triggered something into motion. Like that one kiss changed the world around us, tilting the perpetual axis. Like somehow that one kiss had signified our entire being of life—it didn't.

That kiss meant nothing, and the feelings that formed from within because of it meant nothing. Every time I thought of Maggie, the way her brown hair billowed in the wind, the way her small hands clasped mine, it reminded me of the illness, the death that plagued me. It reminded me of the clock that slowly ticked inside of me.

I was dying, and there was nothing anyone could do. There was no cure, no miracle for someone like me. After all, millions of people lost their loved ones, so what would one more loss be? What would me not dying do for the world? *Nothing.*

Eventually, I would be replaced. The school would get a new student, the teachers would forget I ever existed and Maggie... sweet little Maggie would move on and find someone new. My parents would have another child and life would be normal. *Normal, for everyone but me.*

See, I wouldn't get to live such a lavish life. No, the life I would live would make me wish the cancer had killed me. That it had eaten away at everything that made me who I was. Why, you ask? Simply because the person I was morphing into, the man they were creating me to become—was anything less than death. He was ruthless, angry, and hateful. He thought of no one but himself. He was careless, his needs only being met with sex and violence.

His memories would be wiped away, yet a small girl with red cheeks and brown hair would still find her way into his dreams. He would grow to hate that little girl for not being able to remember the memories of her while driving himself insane wondering where she came from.

He would eventually become one of the world's

best-trained fighters. Genetically mutated to the government's liking. Turned into something he never wanted—something he never should've been.

Now, you see, his legacy, or the memories of who he was, would never be remembered because there was nothing to remember about a twelve-year-old boy who should be dead. No family, friends, or loved ones to care.

He was a killer—and I am he.

one

MAGGIE—THE PAST

I HATED WHEN the other kids laughed at him. They would push and shove him, not even caring he was sick. Sometimes, I wanted to push them back or scream for them to leave him alone. Except I knew no one would listen to me. They never did. Instead, I sat in the background waiting for the moment I could swoop in and care for him.

He was taller than the other kids were—even at the age of sixteen—and just as cute. It didn't matter to me how his skin was almost always ghostly white or how, instead of jeans, he would much rather be wearing something that didn't cling to his body. To me, he was perfect.

"What's a matter, Diesel...? Maggie not make you your breakfast this morning?" Roger, one of the biggest bullies of them all, mocked Diesel. This

was a regular occurrence on the bus. Every morning this same conversation would take place. I was starting to wonder, when would it stop? Diesel ignored him like always and stared out the window. I watched from the seat across from him as Roger sat behind him and shoved his knees into the back of his seat.

Fury grew deep within me, raging like a burning fire. Oh, how I hated what was going on. Diesel had told me many times how me sticking up for him just made things worse for him, and for me. That there was nothing like a girl sticking up for a boy. It was against the rules. Lucky for him and me, I didn't play by the rules. One would say I was a rule breaker.

"Knock it off, Roger," I murmured. Diesel's steel blue eyes turned to mine shooting daggers at me. I could tell by his one single look that I had angered him.

"Awe, what was that you said, Maggie? I couldn't quite hear you, but then again, most of us never do." He belittled me, laughing as his friends joined in the mockery.

"Just leave her alone," Diesel exclaimed giving them the satisfaction they wanted. They wanted him to talk, to stick up for me—for anything—simply because it showed he had a weakness for something... for someone.

"You guys hear this? He wants us to leave Maggie alone." Roger mocked some more, and I did whatever I could not to turn toward Diesel to take in his expression.

You're a weakness to him. They will use you to get to him. I repeated the same words over and over again in my mind.

I became momentarily distracted as I talked myself out of sticking up for him again. So much so, I hadn't noticed Roger had slipped into my seat. I turned, staring into his eyes. They were a dark brown that had most of the girls in the school falling at his feet. All except me. I knew the meanness lingered just under the surface. He was a monster in disguise.

"Maggie..." he hissed as one of his fingers gripped a lock of my hair. A tingle of pain radiated through my scalp as a soft yelp left my lips.

"Leave me alone, Roger." I kept my voice stern and strong not wanting him to think his hair pulling had gotten the best of me.

"Leave you alone...?" he mocked, a sick smile forming on his face. If Roger weren't such a dog, one would consider him cute. He had that beautiful sandy brown hair, and he was tall and played all kinds of sports. His parents could afford it, unlike Diesel's or mine. He was perfect in the eyes of everyone around us, and that's what set him apart. No one expected his behavior.

"Roger, this is taking it a little far." Diesel tried to hide the panic in his voice, but you could tell what Roger was doing was getting to him. It was times like these that even if he had said we weren't friends—because a dying person couldn't make friends with someone in such a short amount of time—I knew I meant something to him.

"*Does it bother you when I touch her, Diesel? Are you jealous?*" Roger taunted, his hand slipping onto my leg. I was wearing a skirt, which was an unfortunate wardrobe choice for the day. I swatted his hand away, only for him to bring it back and grip my thigh hard.

"*Let go of me,*" I growled, growing angrier with every passing second. Roger had never taken it this far. He had never touched me in a physical nature before.

"*Roger, let go of her.*" There was vengeance in Diesel's eyes, and his voice was stronger than I had ever heard it. He moved to the edge of his seat and leaned over gripping Roger by the shoulder.

"*Get your hand the hell off me, cripple...*" Roger rolled his shoulders, forcing Diesel's hand to fall away. He lifted his hand forming a fist as if he were going to hit him. I knew I couldn't allow that to happen, so I tried to distract him. I grabbed Roger's wrist, prying his touch from my thigh, as I watched him lower his raised fist.

"*If you ever get done playing with the crippled boy...*" Roger gazed at Diesel out of the corner of his eye as if to send a warning. "*You know where to find me,*" he whispered the ending of his sentence into my ear causing my hair to stir. I could feel the heat from his breath against my skin, and it made me skin itch. I wanted to sneer at him, tell him I would never give into him, I would never be like one of the many girls I went to school with.

Instead, I turned my attention to the window, clenching my fists while counting to ten. Out of the corner of my eye, I saw him watch me for a mere second, his eyes eating away at my body. Then he slipped from my seat and into his regular seat a ways back.

I released the breath I was holding, allowing fresh oxygen to filter into my lungs. Roger was a monster, the living, breathing kind your parents forgot to tell you about. The kind that had the power to make your life a living hell, day in and day out—and he did just that.

"I told you not to stick up for me." Diesel's voice was right next to me, and as I turned around to see where he was, I came face to face with him. His dark hair was long and slung back in a ponytail. He was looking at me with anger in his eyes, anger I had never seen in him before. A shudder ran through me as I bit my lip unsure of what I should say.

"Well, I told you I wouldn't let them pick on you anymore. They don't know what they're saying. They're dumb." They looked at Diesel as an outcast because he didn't talk to others. But what they didn't realize was him not talking to others had to do with the cancer that surged through his veins. They didn't understand, in Diesel's eyes, there was no point in making memories he may not be here for tomorrow.

"They know what they're saying, Maggie." He scoffed, his attention going back toward the front of the bus as if to make it seem like he wasn't paying an ounce of attention to me.

"You always try to see the good in people; you

always try to protect the weak. What you don't understand is I don't need protecting." He turned back toward me, his eyes boring into mine, willing me to understand what he was saying. The problem was I didn't want to understand—I just wanted to help. I could feel emotions I had never felt before finding their way to the surface.

"You can't save everything. You can't save me," he hissed out. My gaze slid down to his clenched fists and over his body, which was built tightly like a rubber band ready to snap, like a man filled with aggression. I understood his pain though. His anger was evident. I knew he didn't want to be protected, he didn't want even one friend if there was a chance he would die—and there was. Every day since his diagnosis was an extra day given. Friends meant when you died, you would leave someone behind. You would have a reason to feel guilty about your death. He didn't want that.

"I don't want to save you, Diesel," I murmured staring intensely into his eyes. His attention shifted to me, the look in his eyes reminding me of waves crashing against the sand on the beach.

"Yes, yes, you do. You. The doctors. My parents. They all want to save me. Everyone wants me to live—except me." There was so much agony in the words he was saying. It was as if he knew his fate and fighting it was inevitable.

"That isn't true—" My words cut off, as his hand landed on my knee gripping it. He wasn't hurting me, but he easily could have. Even if he was sick, he still held strength behind his touch,

behind his words.

"It is true. Believe me when I say it's true. I know what you all think. I know you assume sticking up for me makes it better, maybe you even think if you're nice to me, when I die, God will grant you something special." He was sneering now, his words forced out between his teeth.

"That's not the p—" My words were cut off again as he squeezed my knee. The pain radiated up my leg, and I bit my lip to stifle the cry that wanted to escape my mouth.

"I don't want to hurt you, Maggie. I don't want to do anything to ruin you, but whatever you think is going on between us, isn't. Whatever help you think you can offer me, you can't. In the end, you're only going to hurt yourself and bring more attention to me. The attention I have no need to seek."

My mind was blank. Like a chalkboard that had been wiped clean. I had nothing to say—at least, nothing that would be worth saying. He didn't care. He didn't want support. Even though it broke my heart to see others beat him with their words and hands, there was nothing I could do to save someone who didn't want to be saved. He was right... I was putting my nose somewhere it wasn't needed. I had been for the past six months now. Since the day when his parents came out and told everyone he had been battling cancer the last four years. We all knew there was something going on. He was missing school all the time, losing weight, and his demeanor had taken a major hit. He hated *everyone and everything.*

"Do you understand me?" he asked softly. His voice caressed my body in a blanket of warmth. He didn't realize the good he could produce, the good he had the chance to bestow upon others.

I nodded my head, willing away the tears that were on the verge of slipping from my eyes. Be strong. Give him what he wants.

"Good," he said satisfied with the conversation. His hand slipped from my knee, as I had to force myself not to rub it from the pain.

The rest of the bus ride consisted of me sitting in the far corner of my seat staring out the window pretending his body heat wasn't what I was feeling next to me. I forced myself not to lash out and say something to him—something that would only push him further away.

As we pulled up to the school, and the bus came to a stop, my heart felt as if it were going to beat out of my chest.

"Remember what I said, Maggie." His voice was a whisper in the wind as he got out of the seat and pushed in line to get off the bus.

He said nothing more to me, and even as he looked at me now, I knew he wouldn't. At least not after this conversation. The words he had said would be the last he would ever speak to me unless I provoked him.

I couldn't force myself to move. It was as if I had lost all control of my body.

Eventually, I found my bearings and slipped into the back of the line, my mind drifting to

Diesel's words. I can't be saved...

Maybe he didn't think he could be saved. Maybe he didn't think he was worth it, but I did. I saw it when I looked into his eyes. I felt it whenever he would touch me, and somewhere in the depths of his soul, even though he was telling me he couldn't be saved... in his soul, he was screaming for someone to save him.

Diesel was worth saving—he just didn't know it yet.

two

MAGGIE—THE PRESENT

"Maggie." I could hear my name being called from across the room, but I still failed to acknowledge the voice saying it. Either that or I didn't care to acknowledge it. I would go with the latter of the two.

"Maggie, open your fucking ears. I need that paperwork on my desk ASAP!" The voice yelled again, their footsteps growing closer until they stopped in front of my desk. Oh, I knew that voice. It belonged to my boss's son. The same son who had caused me great pain in my younger years. He hadn't changed—not one bit, unless you considered growing into a bigger dickwad than he previously was. He was still a fucking bully, a piece of shit asshole who felt like he controlled everything—including me.

"Okay," I finally said, hoping my one-word response would get him to leave my desk. To say I hated my job was a fucking understatement. A huge one at that. I more than hated it. If it weren't a means of income, or a way to answers I desperately wanted, I would've cut ties with the place years ago. I couldn't though. I needed the money, and I wanted answers almost more than I wanted my next breath.

I never wanted to work for PGI Corp, but they were one of the biggest growing companies in our town, and they were offering jobs to anyone willing to work. Plus, I had an inspiration for coming into this shit hole every day. I had a memory, a piece of my heart that forced me to work here.

Someone long ago told me they didn't need saving, and since that day, I told myself I would do whatever I could to come up with a cure. That person motivated me to push my efforts so no one would have to go through death and loss ever again.

"Okay? That's all you're going to fucking say?" Roger was the only one who could actually get away with swearing in the office. He said *fuck* like it was going out of style. His vocabulary included more swear words than it did regular words.

"Yes, okay. As in, I will have the papers to you as soon as I can get online." My voice was monotone as it always was. I would never give him the satisfaction of knowing every word that came from his mouth made me want to barf into the nearest trash can.

"Good, because I have something else for you to

do when you bring the papers in." He wiggled his eyebrows at me as he leaned over my desk and into my personal space. *Remember why you're doing this, Maggie. Remember.* I had to repeat this to myself every day, at least three times daily. It was the only thing that stopped me from running for the hills, from running out of this place and never turning the fuck around.

"Great," I whispered to myself, turning on my computer as he walked away. I watched the screen light up as my thoughts drifted to my family and everything they had done for me. My parents had paid for my college tuition. I was more than grateful since they didn't have much. My father held a good job, but the way the world was nowadays made going to college almost impossible. Only the richest or smartest people were accepted into schools. The fact I was wasting a degree in Pharmaceutical Studies by working for someone like Roger didn't sit well with them. They wanted to see me do something with my life. Working a desk job wasn't bettering the community or my own life.

As my computer booted up, I watched Kandace a couple of desks down from me flirting with one of the new hires. I smiled sincerely at her ballsy attitude. She had balls—hell, I think she had bigger balls than most of the men who worked in this place.

Her eyes met mine as I watched her work her moves. She a natural flirt, a social butterfly most would say. She batted her eyelashes and flashed him a smile before stepping away from his

PROJECT: k i l l e r

desk and sashaying her way over to me.

"You're still taking orders from that asshat in a suit..." Kandace giggled softly, leaning her ass against my desk.

"If you mean the asshat who's my boss, then yes, of course, I'm listening to him." I typed my password into the computer and waited for my email to load.

"A couple of people from the office and I are headed into the city tonight. We're going to hit up one of those new clubs on the strip," she added innocently. I knew where she was going with this. She had been bitching more than usual about my lack of being a wing woman. The thing was—I just wasn't feeling it. Dating wasn't my thing and sitting at a bar drinking away my sorrows wasn't either.

I would much rather be at home in my sweats, reading a book, and drinking a glass of wine... "I know what you're getting at, Kandace, and the answer is the same as it was last week." She frowned, a pout showing on her face.

"You always say that. You always say you would rather have your nose stuck in a book, but since you never go out, how would you know what is fun and what isn't?" She was questioning me, attempting to find a flaw in my excuse. Anything to get me to leave the confines of my home.

"Very funny, Kandace, but I know your methods of persuasion, and since I don't swing that way, it's not going to work..." Her pout turned into a cheesy smile.

"Well, I tried. Doesn't matter anyway. You're

P a g e | **28**

coming out tonight even if I have to come to your house and get you myself." She glared at me, and it was in that glare I knew she was serious.

Fuck. She wasn't kidding. She would come and get me. I pondered on the actual thought of going out for a moment as I skimmed the emails in my inbox.

"We'll see, Kandace. There isn't any guarantee though."

"There is always a guarantee with Kandace. I'll see you at eight, whore." Then she was up and walking back to her own desk, and I was staring at an email that had just popped into my inbox from Roger.

I printed off the documents he wanted *ASAP* and headed to the printer to pick them up before swinging by his office. On my walk to the printer, my mind drifted to Roger and the company I was working for. It was obvious Roger would turn into his father one day. Roger's father was a filthy rich man, hell-bent on owning everyone and everything in this town. I knew the kind of person Roger was, and honestly, I couldn't see such a mean and evil person running a company that went out of their way to find cures for cancer. It was a complete and utter contradiction. His family running and owning a company that cared for others loved ones was just against everything I knew of Roger.

I pushed all the horrible thoughts to the back of my mind as I focused in on Roger's door. I stared at it blankly for a moment before knocking on it softly and waiting for him to say come in.

You never walked into Roger's office unannounced. I remember the last assistant he had ended up being fired and escorted out on the spot. He was very secretive about his work. Whatever went on in his office was his business and his business alone.

"Come in." His voice was deep, and as I pushed the door open and walked into the room, I could see the entire city before me. He had the best view in the building. One that looked out into the robust city. I focused on the view, knowing very well that his eyes were glued to my every movement. I could feel his gaze penetrating every orifice of my body.

"I see you're doing much better at following orders today." He smiled, but it wasn't genuine. It was as fake as Tammy's tits in Office C. Who was Tammy, you ask? Oh, his most recent fuck. The newest intern in the building, and the most open about her friends with benefits relationship with Roger.

"Here's your paperwork you asked for." I dismissed his comment, not wanting to engage in a ridiculous conversation about something I couldn't care less about. Instead, I turned on my heels to leave only to be stopped when I heard his throat clear behind me. I wanted to turn around and lash out, to make him understand what he said to me meant nothing.

"Maggie..." Every time he said my name, it caused my stomach to revolt. He was just as sinister now as he was in high school.

"Yes," I said between clenched teeth with my

j.l. beck

face turned away from him. I hadn't ever truly hated anyone in my entire life, but Roger was the exception. If he were dying in a burning building, I would sit and watch. Maybe even bring stuff to make s'mores.

"We all know why you took a job here. It's not as if you actually care for the company, but more so what it can do for you." I took a deep breath, the room seemingly growing smaller as air filled my lungs only to be released like a deflated balloon a moment later. *Breathe. Deep breaths.*

"That..." Was that true? I had never admitted to such a thing. Sweat formed on my palms. I hated feeling as if I were trapped without an escape route.

"Don't even say it's not true when we both know it is. You took this job for that fucking crippled kid."

Crippled kid... Don't make him eat his words. Kill him with kindness.

"He had a name." I forced the words from my mouth. I didn't want to talk about *him*. His death wasn't fair to anyone—not his family, not to me, or to him.

"Whatever, his name doesn't matter. Not anymore at least. What does is the fact you took a job working for me, yet it seems as if you would much rather not be here most days." I could hear his footsteps across the marble flooring, my heartrate rising with every step.

"I love my job..." I lied, trying not to stutter over my words. I hated my job, but I hated Roger and what he reminded me of more. *Hurt. Pain.*

A deep robust laugh filled the room. "That is the biggest fucking lie I have ever heard." His hot breath was on the back of my neck. I should've turned around. I should've told him to leave me alone.

"Fine. I'm here for him, and one day, I will be on the team that helps find a cure for the cancer he had. He wasn't just crippled, Roger. He was sick. He was dying." I smarted off, openly admitting my faults as I turned around to face him not realizing how close he truly was to me. I took a wobbly step back wanting to separate us, my legs feeling like jelly.

Roger's hand reached out and gripped my chin hard, pulling my face into his. There was a sick fire in his eyes, one that said he would hurt me if he had to. Men like him weren't afraid of someone like me getting in their way.

"You think you have everyone fooled, that no one will discover you for what you really are." He was seething.

What was he talking about? I hadn't ever tried to dissect what Roger had to say only because he was wrong most, if not all, of the time. His motives were always to protect his empire or to make others suffer. He was out to benefit no one but himself.

"I have no one fooled," I gritted out, the hold he had on my jaw growing tighter. I winced as his fingers dug deeper into my skin. His face leaned into mine as his eyes lingered on my lips before rising to my own. He wanted to kiss me. I knew it. I felt it in his stare and in his touch. He wanted me, but he knew he could never have me. No one could because I was taken. Even with him no longer here, he still lived and breathed in me... in my heart, and I would not betray him with his enemy.

"You're right... You have no one fooled simply because they can see through your ulterior motives. Watch your back, Maggie. You might find more than just a knife in it."

He released me, shoving me away from him. His threat lingered in my mind long after I had got my footing and walked out of his office. Rubbing at my jaw, I attempted not to draw attention to myself. That would only make it worse.

Instead, I went to my desk and kept myself busy by looking at various articles about Diesel's cancer. He had a rare brain tumor, stage four at the time of his death. It was inoperable, meaning there was nothing they could do to save him. They had given him months to live, which turned into years. Many said it was a miracle he had held on for as long as he did. I felt there was always something else lingering under the surface. A hidden reasoning or an answer.

My fingers pounded on the keys for hours, doing my research as I did every day. This wasn't my job, though. I was to shuffle papers in and out of Roger's office. I was basically his assistant without the title or pay raise. My plan was to get into the labs and out of the office. There was nothing here for me and having been here for six months, I hadn't discovered much of anything. PGI's database was locked down tighter than Fort Knox. Codes were needed for just about everything, and I wasn't so desperate for answers that I would sleep with someone or lie and cheat to get them. I had to do this the right way.

"Maggie," Kandace said in a motherly tone. I looked up from my keyboard and gave her a look that said I was working and to go away.

"Kandace."

"I saw you come out of Roger's office earlier. Is everything okay?" Kandace had always been concerned about my relationship with Roger. He bullied me in school, and just when I thought I would be able to get away from him, here I was working under him.

"Yeah, just the typical shit that he puts me through. I can never just go into his office and give him his daily spreadsheets." I kept my voice hushed. There were office rats all around us. People who would turn around and tell him anything and everything that took place out on the floor. They thought it would gain them more money or freedom. Some did it just because they could.

"You were rubbing at your face when you came out. Don't lie to me and tell me it's nothing, Maggie. If he's fucking with you again, then I will find out and do something about it."

I smiled to myself. God, how had I been blessed with such a great friend? She was someone who would kick any and everyone's ass if I asked her to do it.

"It's nothing. At least nothing different from the norm. You know why I'm here, Kandace. I want to get into the labs and see what kind of cures and drugs they're coming up with," I whispered to her, my eyes scanning the room. One would think moving up in the company would be something relatively normal, something that could easily be talked about in the workplace. Except it wasn't. At least not here. Moving up to a new position was never something openly discussed. If you moved up, you just quietly disappeared.

Any promotion in the company was top secret. If you ever made it out of this sector of the building, then you knew something no one else did. I had to make it happen. I had to find out what was going on—if not for the families who were suffering from death, grief, and loss, then for Diesel.

"It's been seven years. Seven years, Maggie. It's time to move on. It's time to let it go. He died. He's not coming back, and if you keep thinking like you are, it's going to get you killed."

Kandace's concern was cute but entirely unnecessary. I had it all under control. Maybe if I kept telling myself that it would start to feel that way.

"He might be dead, but I made him a promise. I told him I would try to help find a cure for his cancer. I wasn't lying to him seven years ago, and I'm not going back on my word now. I understand your concerns, but I'm not doing anything wrong."

The look of shock on her face astounded me. Did she really feel as if what I was doing was wrong? That wanting to stand by my word was wrong?

"Davis." Roger's angry voice met our ears. Everyone turned to see what the issue was, including myself.

"Sir..." Davis stumbled over his words as he got into a standing position pushing from his desk as if he had just been told to jump. *What the fuck is going on?*

"Why don't you tell the rest of the staff what happens when you try to make a fool of this company? Of the company my father spent years building from the ground up." There was a glint of something I had never seen in Roger's eyes. A need for blood—for death.

"Sir... Can we talk about—" Davis tried adding, but it did no good. Roger waved in security as his hand landed on Davis's shoulder.

"No, we cannot talk about this. Once it's found out you're here for yourself and not the company, then it becomes a problem. You made us believe you had the company's best interest at heart, but you didn't. So, that means you lied, and I don't do well with liars. We're a team, Davis, but you aren't a team player. If we all did whatever we wanted, for whatever reason, this company wouldn't be what it is. Let alone exist."

"I promise it won't happen again..." Davis pleaded, sweat beading on his forehead as he clasped his hands together.

"I know it won't, Davis, and neither will any of these people make the same mistake as you. Listen up. This is what happens to you when you disobey this company. When you think you can use it for your own benefits." Every word that came out of Roger's mouth was spat directly at me. His eyes drilled into mine as the guards came in, pulling Davis from the room as if he never meant a damn thing to them.

With a smile, Roger walked away... His eyes bore into mine, and his threat still rang in my ears. For once, it was starting to hit me. The good of doing this might not outweigh the bad.

Kandace was right.

I could very well be signing my own death certificate.

three

KILLER—THE PRESENT

"WHEN YOU THINK about dying, what do you think it will be like?" Her question rang in my ears. Her soft, delicate voice wrapped me in warmth like I had never felt before.

To say I wasn't human would be true. I wasn't. At least, not since they pumped me full of drugs. They morphed me into this killing machine, but now I was free. Free of the chains, the bars, and the people. Never again would I find myself in confinement.

My thoughts drifted back to the things they made us do. The killing, the fights they caused between us. They wanted to control us, to make us into their own little lab rats. None of us truly understood the need they had for us. Some of us were injected with drugs to alter the human DNA while others were trained to fight.

"You were talking in your sleep again," Jaxon, my right-hand man, said from his bunk. We were in hiding having just escaped the facility where they were holding us. They thought we were weak. They thought wrong. I remember wrapping my hands around the doctor's throat as he tried to shoot me up with a tranquilizer. It almost made me laugh.

The memories of bones crunching, the gurgling of blood in his throat, his eyes popping out of his head from the pressure of my hand squeezing, and the way his face turned purplish blue from lack of oxygen as bruises formed from underneath my fingers—it all fed me. Fed me to find vengeance. The people who had created this drug and administered it to us would die. I would make sure their blood stained my hands one way or another.

"Sorry," I offered stretching in my bed. Our beds were small, but they were beds. We had never been given anything as soft... let alone a pillow or mattress. Those things were lavish and unknown to even us.

"Don't be. I know what you're going through." Jaxon offered his sympathy, even when he knew I wouldn't take it. He knew what I wanted him to know, which wasn't very much. Most of us had no recollection of who we were, what we were doing, or where we had come from. *Except me.* I had memories. I could feel the pain and hurt in those memories, which told me once I had been sick. Once I had been dying and there was no hope. Yet, here I was, breathing and living. How I had come to live and thrive was unknown. Something told me PGI knew more than they were ever letting on.

I grunted in return as I pulled my long brown hair into a ponytail. I had plans to get my hands bloody today. That wasn't changing. I had one desire, one reason my heart was still beating, and it was to take out anyone I could who would have answers.

After all they had done to us, they deserved death. Fuck, it would be their last dying wish by the time I got done with them.

"My body's itching for a kill, Jaxon." I rolled my shoulders and cracked my knuckles. We had been at the secret compound for months now. The building was a brick structure built into the ground five-floors deep. To the naked eye, it would be seen as a newer apartment building. If they entered it, they would have another thing coming. Behind its walls lay killers, genetically mutated males capable of far more than just death. One look could strike fear so deep some would lose their minds.

"Mine, too. It feels like it's been days since I ripped that nurse's fucking throat out as she screamed. My cock was hard the entire time I did it, too." He smiled like a sick fuck. Society was made to think what he had just described was bad, and it was. What they were doing to us was just as bad, though. We had learned that an eye for an eye was how justice would be served. Do to us only what you wish to be done to you.

"Killer. Jaxon." Gauge said our names with authority in his voice. Gauge was someone you could consider to be the President of the escapees. He was still in touch with his humanity for the most part. I had yet to see a time when he truly lost his shit.

"Gauge," I greeted him, my voice gruff. I needed to fuck or spill blood. *Something.* Blood spilling quenched the thirst of the slaughterer I had become, and since fucking was an opportunity that wasn't given to us often, spilling blood was my favorite.

Women shied away from us, and those who did want in on the sex couldn't handle it. We were savages in everything we did. Fucking and fighting were our best outlets for anger. Both always ended in blood.

"You look like a bear that's been poked one too many times," Gauge joked. I didn't smile. Hell, I didn't find it even remotely fucking funny.

"Want to hear a joke?" Her voice entered my mind as a flash of a memory hit me. My fists clenched as I gripped at the bed sheet. The muscles in my stomach clenched as I forced myself to hold onto every second of it.

She had brown hair that flowed down her back freely. Big brown eyes that sparkled as she smiled at something I had said. She was saying something to me, her mouth moving, but I was unable to hear it... She was fading out...

"Killer." Gauge's voice was the first I heard, and it only made my anger worse. Who was she, and why the fuck did I have memories of a life I didn't remember living?

"Get the fuck away from me," I growled. I was on the verge of ripping the whole fucking room apart. My body was shaking as I shot out of bed.

"Killer. Stop. Calm down." Gauge's voice rang in my ears, but his words meant nothing to me. It was as if my mind and body weren't connected. I wouldn't be able to stop the destruction I would cause until I found answers. I needed them. So fucking badly.

Blood. Bathe in the blood of your enemies, the little voice in my head said. I smiled like the devil at the mere thought of killing—slaughtering.

I made my way up from the fourth floor climbing all four flights of stairs without a single bead of sweat forming. I was made this way. I was made to be indestructible.

Finding the nearest exit, I pushed out into the open alleyway that sat next to the building. It was time to hunt. To prey upon those who deserved it most. A piece of who I was, the one who clung to my humanity, the one who held onto the memory of that girl—disappeared. In its place was a man who would kill without even a thought. When I looked at the world through these eyes, I saw mass chaos and the need to rectify, to deliver my revenge. There was no mercy, compassion, or caring.

There was only death, revenge, and blood.

With my heart beating out of my chest, I lifted my nose into the air, searching for my next kill. In a city like this, rapist, criminals, and other disgusting beings, I could find my next kill without any effort.

I scoured the alleyways until I stumbled upon a

man cornering a woman. Her shrill cries could be heard from a block over, yet everyone continued to pass by ignoring the problem. That was the issue with these people. They didn't care about those who were being preyed upon. They just kept going on, minding their own business, acting as if they hadn't even seen it. That's how they were raised—to turn a blind eye to those being hurt.

A growl escaped my throat as the man who held the woman against the wall turned toward me.

"Want to join?" he asked, his hand slipping under her shirt. Tears had started streaming down the woman's face, her lips swollen, and one of her eyes black.

"Yes," I said with an animalistic sound now present in my voice. My body pleaded with me to snatch him up by the throat. To crush his windpipe, to make him beg for his next breath. His smile grew bigger in the dim lighting. He thought I wanted to join him in the raping of the woman he had taken captive. The very woman he was beating on.

"Roger, stop. Please stop." Another memory hit me. The same girl crying and pleading with someone to stop. What were they doing to her?

Rage consumed me as I pushed the memory away and crossed the alleyway a second later. I gripped the man by his jacket pulling him into my face as the woman slumped against the building.

Then my hands were around his throat. My teeth were clenched like the beast I was as I squeezed with all my might. I had no need to punch or to kick. I had learned cutting off air supply was the best way to go. Fewer marks, less screaming, and it gave them a chance to stare into my eyes as I watched the life leave their body.

The man's eyes bulged out as I squeezed tighter and tighter. I could hear the shattering of bones and feel the pulsing of blood through his still beating heart. My muscles burned as heat bloomed in my veins stirring the fiery beast within.

I closed my eyes as I felt his skin breaking. I felt his blood marring my hands, the warmth of his death radiated through me causing a europium of emotions to form. As I released his lifeless body to the ground, I focused on my breathing... rubbing the blood of my enemy into my hands.

The shallow cries of the woman could be heard in the back of my mind, but I hesitated. Making sure she was okay wasn't something I should do. I was a monster. I could kill her. One kill was never enough. *Never.* I could feel it already, the need to deprive someone of life filling me to the brim. I needed to get away from this woman, and I needed to do it now before she became my next victim.

As I took my first step away from the woman, a voice entered my mind cutting off all movement.

"You're so smart, Diesel."

"Stop," I screamed, my hands clawing at my head. I wanted to rip the memories from my mind. To throw them away. I was paralyzed, a victim to my own memories, my own body.

"Are you flirting with me?" She smiled as I placed my hand on hers. Her brown eyes were so warm and vibrant.

"Stop. I can't take it anymore." I fell to my knees. The strongest most-indestructible man on the planet had one singular weakness that he wasn't even aware of, someone he had no name for—just mere memories of his life.

Either I was going crazy, having been dosed one too many times, or I was starting to remember small glimpses of my life before I became the man I am now. All I knew was that neither one was good for me. Remembering my previous life had the chance of pulling me into a deeper, darker world. Not remembering would drive me insane. I was damned if I did and damned if I didn't.

"Killer, stand in your cell, or I'll have to send someone in who will make you." I gritted my teeth. *I would love to see them try. Rage stirred inside of me, the idea of getting my hands on them again. I loved the feel of their bones breaking, the rage that would consume me at that moment.*

"5..." He was counting down to his own death.

"4..." He had no idea what I wanted to do to him, but he was going to find out soon.

"3..." I cracked my knuckles and waited for them to enter...

"2... Back up..." His voice was shallow, almost not meeting my ears. Adrenaline pumped through my veins, and a smile pulled at my lips.

"1..." The doors to my cell opened, and in they walked with their tranquilizers and doping drugs. I had lashed out before they got the chance to touch me, swiping my hand across the chest of the man who was closest to me as I dug my fingers

into his flesh. Blood sprayed from his wound, splattering against the wall and other men with him. I felt nothing for killing him. He would be replaced tomorrow by someone just as dumb as he was.

"Killer..." I could hear someone yelling just as a dart hit me square in the chest. I smiled knowing I, at the very least, had gotten my point across.

four

MAGGIE

TODAY WAS YET another bad day. Roger had ended up beating the shit out of Diesel in gym class, and somehow, I had known something was wrong once he didn't show up to class. I excused myself to the restroom but headed straight to the boys locker room. There he stood leaning against the far wall of the bathroom his arms clenching his midsection. His eyes grew large as he took me in.

"You shouldn't be in here, Maggie." His voice was weak, he was sweating profusely, and he looked more exhausted than I had ever seen him.

"You didn't show up to American Lit, so I assumed something was wrong. Looks like I was right." I tried to keep my tone out of the smart-ass area, but it didn't work. From the look on his face, he didn't seem to find it funny either.

"I don't need your help. How many fucking times do I have to tell you that?" He was as livid as he was most times I came running to his rescue. Honestly, I couldn't tell you what it was that made me come back for more. Every time I helped him, it was like being stung by a bee. Every time I stuck my fingers into the warm honey, I would get stung. Eventually, the pain subsided and didn't feel nearly as bad as going without the honey. I guess I looked at Diesel like that.

"Looks like you're going to have to tell me one more time because I didn't hear it the last thousand other times," I joked, walking over to him. He stared at me a darkness settling into his eyes. This was the part where he would try to threaten me. Try to convince me how being friends was a weakness he couldn't afford and if I didn't stop, he would hurt me.

It was always a lie. I could call his bluff by now. Sometimes, I would think the tumor was finally getting to him, that he was actually losing parts of his mind only because he would tell me the same thing every single time I did something for him.

"Don't," he growled as I reached a hand out to steady him. His clothes clung to his sweaty body as a groan sounded from deep within his chest.

"Just let me help you," I said ignoring his shoves. He was weaker than I was—that much I knew.

"I said no," he yelled, his voice hurting my ears. His hand reached out and grabbed my arm

gripping it in a manner that would've scared me—should've scared me.

"I said yes." I gritted my teeth gripping him under the arm as I lead him to the bench. His grip on my arm slacked as I sat him down, his head leaning back against the tiled wall.

"Go back to class, Maggie. We go through this every fucking day. Every. Fucking. Day. You tell me I need you, I tell you I don't. When are you going to understand this infatuation you have with me is going to get you hurt?"

Infatuation? What was he talking about?

"Infatuation? Are you kidding me? I help you because it's the right thing to do and because regardless of how the others treat you, I know you deserve more than just to be picked on and beaten. I mean, look at you now..."

"Fucking Christ, Mags, just leave. Leave while you still can. I'm dying. Hell, I should already be dead. I'm losing my mind, my memories, and my thoughts every single day. Every breath I take, every morning I wake up, I'm that much closer to death. So please cut the shit and walk away. It's been years, and I'm barely hanging on by a thread. A fucking thread, Maggie. A. THREAD!!!" he bellowed. His face was red in frustration as I took a step away from him, my back hitting the lockers. I had seen him angry. I had seen him cry, but I had never seen his hate turned on me.

"I just wanted to help you," I mumbled. It was the plan the whole time—to be a friend to him when he needed one most.

"Don't. Stop helping. Stop caring. Stop it all. Because if you don't stop, I will force you to stop." He stood, breathing heavily.

I wasn't sure I could handle a day without Diesel. Maybe that was the problem he was getting at. I was using helping him as an excuse to hide the fact I was already attached to him. He never wanted me to get attached to him because you can't attach yourself to death. He wasn't trying to hurt me. He was trying to protect me.

I jolted awake, a sheen of sweat covering me. Fuck, another memory. Another nightmare. I felt as if I would be plagued by them for the rest of my life. As if not knowing what happened to him was my own personal hell.

He died, Maggie. He fucking died, and there was nothing you or anyone else could do.

Tears threatened to spring from my eyes. I loved Diesel with every piece of myself. I just wish I would have been strong enough to tell him how I felt much sooner than I did. That way, we could have spent more time loving one another, showing each other in every aspect how deep that love ran. Suddenly, my cell phone started to ring. My mind was a boggled mess as I searched the bedsheets for it.

My hand landed on it as I pulled it out from under my pillow. Kandace. Fudge sickles. I hit the answer key and waited for the bitching to ensue.

"Don't tell me you were taking a nap..." she yelled into the phone.

"I..."

"Actually, you better have been taking a nap. You're pulling an all-nighter." She interrupted me not even giving me a chance to speak.

"Thanks for telling me what I'm doing tonight," I said in a smartass tone.

"No problem. You best be ready in T-minus thirty minutes. I will be at your apartment to pick you up then." Thirty minutes? She had to be kidding.

"Really, I just wanted to stay in and—"

"Read a fucking book. I know, I know." She finished my sentence for me. I needed to come up with better excuses.

"Whatever. I'll be ready," I said giving up. There wasn't any point. I had no other excuses. It was time for me to socialize a bit, to step out of my comfort zone.

"Good," was all she said before hanging up on me. I slithered from my bed and walked to the bathroom, pulling on a pair of skinny jeans along the way. It was only eight. I had slept for three hours... crashing the moment I had walked into my loft apartment.

Finding a sparkly blouse, I slipped it on and then pulled my black boots on. I tamed my dark brown hair by putting it in a braid and applied a small amount of makeup. My brown eyes reflected back at me, and I felt as if I didn't know myself.

The more and more I thought about what had happened with Roger, and what Kandace had said, the more it dawned on me that maybe I wasn't really doing the right thing. There were other ways

PROJECT: k i l l e r

to help find a cure for something. You didn't have to go into a highly secretive corporation, get into their labs, and find out what it was they were doing that no one else was.

Was it actually worth it to endanger my life, my future of getting an answer for something like this? Then again, what were they hiding? People didn't just threaten others without an intention of protecting something.

A pounding sounded on the door just as I walked from the bathroom to the nightstand to grab my phone. Wow, for the first time ever, Kandace is early. Walking to the door, I pulled it open.

Kandace stood before me decked out in one of the sexiest outfits I had ever seen her wear. Her blonde hair was curled in banana curls, long ringlets falling down her back. She was wearing a black corsage top with red lace embodied through it. Paired with it were a denim mini skirt and a pair of killer black heels. She looked far from the clubbing kind of gal.

"Are you done judging me?" She smirked, her voice holding a tone of amusement. It astonished me how I had become such good friends with her. We were polar opposites in every single way.

"Never. You're going to hell just for wearing that little piece of clothing right there," I joked pointing at her top. Her tits were all but falling out of the top. Yeah, she was getting lucky tonight.

"As long as there are hot as fuck men there, I'm okay with it." She smirked.

"Oh, they'll be something hot there. I don't

P a g e | 54

know that it'll be men though." I giggled. I felt like I had already had an entire bottle of liquor. It had to be the nap.

"Well, you act like you're getting summoned to heaven, child. Do you ever show your body off?" She was teasing me in a bitch kind of way. It didn't matter to me what Kandace thought. I would wear whatever I wanted, how I wanted.

"Yes, Sister Kandace. Now, let's get the hell out of here." I ushered her out the door grabbing all my shit along the way. Tonight was going to be stellar. All I had to do was push the thoughts of him to the back of my mind.

***

Music blasted from the speakers of the club so hard I could feel the beat of the music in my bones. Strobe lights covered the dance floor in every color imaginable as we made our way over to the bar. My eyes caught on everything in the dim lighting. It was as if I was under a spell. I had been missing a lot.

"What do you want to drink?" Kandace yelled into my ear over the music. I wasn't sure what I wanted to drink. I hadn't been out drinking in a long ass time. The closest I got to enjoying alcohol was a glass of wine every now and then, and this place—yeah, it didn't look like it served wine.

Instead, I shrugged my shoulders unsure of what to get. As I gazed around the room at all the people dancing and talking, I forgot about my drink.

"Here, slut." Kandace shoved a glass into my hands. It looked like murky ocean water, and I was unsure if I even wanted to bring my nose near it let alone my lips.

"What the hell is this?" I asked still looking at the glass sideways.

"It's called LA Water. Some of the bitches at the end of the bar were drinking it. I didn't know what to get you so I just went with it." She shrugged taking a sip from her glass, which looked somewhat appetizing.

I brought my nose to the edge of the glass to smell it. The aroma of liquor and sweet fruit hit my nostrils. She had to be fucking crazy if she thought I would drink this. You could smell the hangover on this thing.

"What are you drinking?" I questioned. Hers looked like a frozen margarita but better. I wondered if she would trade beverages with me.

"Mine is called a Cocksucker in honor of all the assholes I have to deal with at work." She smiled around the straw in her mouth, and once she took notice of my not so drunk state, her look turned to a glare.

"Drink, Mags. It's not that bad. If those bitches can handle it, then you know you can. I've seen you sling back whiskey shots... It's not that bad." I wanted to laugh. She was right. Back in the day, we had gotten into my parents alcohol, and eventually, I became one of the most notorious shot drinkers in high school.

"Ugh, fine, but if I'm drunk tomorrow... and it carries into Sunday, then you're explaining to Roger why I'm not at work," I growled bringing the cold beverage to my lips. The coolness was relief that was much needed.

As the first drop of alcohol touched my tongue, an explosion of flavor went off in my mouth. There was no strong taste, just a fruitiness that was almost addicting. Before I knew it, the whole thing had been downed.

"Slow down, Cowboy. I need you to leave this place on your feet, not on a stretcher." Kandace halted me from ordering another drink. I wanted to pout. Was the drink already affecting me?

"Whatever. I'm a big girl, Kandace." I walked around her and up the edge of the bar where the 'bitches' were sitting. Their attention was on a group of youngish looking men in the back booth.

I told the bartender what I wanted and then averted my attention back to the table. At it sat four gigantic men. Their faces were covered in shadows, but even from this distance, I could tell they were bigger dudes.

"Yeah, Jaxon always comes here... He fucked me once but then said he couldn't anymore." One of the girls said, sipping her drink, and eyeing him up like a piece of meat.

"What about his friend... Killer?" the blonde asked with a glint of curiosity in her eyes. I wanted to roll my own eyes at them and their apparent need to pick men up at the club.

"No clue. I mean, his name is Killer. That alone

should scare you away. He doesn't really say anything, and he doesn't interact with any of the other ladies," the brunette went on. The bartender handed me my drink, and I turned around to face the dance floor my eyes still lingering toward the booth of men. Why couldn't I just go dance or something? Why did I feel the need to stare at them?

Taking a gulp from my drink while praying it would give me some type of liquid courage, I watched one of the men get up. His body reminded me of Hulk without the green. His hair was in a man bun, if that was even possible, and his eyes immediately met mine. My breath faltered, and my heart beat out of my chest. It couldn't be. It had to be the lighting or my eyes playing tricks on me.

There was no fucking way Diesel could be standing across the room from me.

five

KILLER

I HATED CLUB nights. Scouting for the piece of shit lab assitants and other workers of the Corporation. The music was loud, the chicks never shut the fuck up, and the booze did nothing to alleviate the monster inside of my head.

"I need to take a leak," I mumbled to Jaxon, who had chick number two on his lap. Greg told us going out in public wasn't a good idea. He feared that if someone noticed us, someone from our past, it could cause problems. By problems, he meant they would have to be taken care of—which I had no problem with. If there was someone from my past who saw me and knew me, I would gladly take them out.

After all, if they truly loved me, then they wouldn't have let me suffer. I got up from the booth, pushing past Savage and Yankee. I had just stepped out of the booth and onto the carpeted floor when I felt someone staring at me. Immediately, my eyes lifted to meet a very shocked, but slightly timid pair of dark brown eyes. I could practically hear her heart beating out of her chest.

She clutched the glass in her hand as if it were a lifeline to reality. I didn't have time to figure out what she was staring at or what she wanted. Hell, she could just be someone who wanted to have a one-night stand with a beast. There were many of those crazy fucking people out there.

Yet, as I took a step away from her, I could feel my own heart rate spike. My palms began to sweat, and my eyes flickered around the room. What the fuck was wrong with me. Ignoring the tugging that I felt in my chest, I hustled to the bathroom. Pushing past a couple, who were all but fucking in the hallway, I made my way to the men's bathroom.

It wasn't until I was done and washing my hands that a piercing pain in my head hit me.

Brown hair. Brown eyes. A dazzling smile. She was a breath of fresh air on a hot summer day. I shook my head fiercely, willing more to slip from my mind. How could it do this to me? How could I only remember bits and pieces of my life? I clenched the soap dispenser and didn't release it until I heard the snapping of plastic.

Deep-rooted chaos was going off inside of my head. It felt like an atomic bomb was about to go off, and I couldn't hold on any longer. Opening the bathroom door, I pushed through the masses of people. I came to a stop when I felt a small form run head-on into me. I clenched my fists forcing myself not to reach out and touch them. I was feeling violent. There was no saying it would just be a simple removal—maybe of their heart or intestines.

"Oh, I'm so, so—" The young woman's voice cut off as she looked up at me. Up close, I could really see her. It was the woman looking at me before I ran off to the bathroom. Was she following me? My blood boiled, and my body begged for some alleviation of the hate. Calmly as I could, I reached out and grabbed her by the shoulder slamming her into the nearby wall.

"Why're you following me?" My voice wasn't my own. Then again, I didn't know what I used to sound like. Her eyes grew wide, full of shock and fear. I could practically see the lie forming in her mind. I wanted to smile, but instead, I wrapped my hand around her throat. Leaning into her body, I caught her scent. She smelt delicious, like chocolate and strawberries.

"Listen really carefully to what I'm about to say to you..." I whispered in her ear taking notice of the way her body responded to my own. Her heart rate accelerated telling me she was scared, but there was something else there.

"I wasn't following you, I swear. I was—"

"Shhhh..." I gripped her around the throat tighter. I had killed women. Not that I had wanted too, but in the moment of rage, I did what I had to. Most of them deserved it.

"You're lying. I can tell. I can hear the spike in your pulse, the way your eyes rolled around as if you were searching your mind for an explanation. The fact it took you a moment to answer me when it was a simple yes or no question." I lifted my head to look into her eyes.

My hand wanted to grip her harder. To bring the lies to the surface without asking questions. Yet, I couldn't allow it. Something held me back, and that just made me even more fucking angry.

"I... I thought I recognized you." She stuttered over her words. My eyes drifted down to her red glossy lips. She was beautiful. Almost as beautiful as *her*. The girl in my memories. Fuck, I needed to stop. *Stop thinking about it.* I told myself.

"You think you know me? Who the fuck is it that you work for?" I growled, my fingers digging into her throat. She reached up, her small hands prying at my fingers to stop. She was begging me with her eyes because she couldn't do so with her words. Forcing myself to ease off, I allowed a breath of oxygen to enter her lungs.

"I work for no one. I just thought I knew you. Obviously, I don't." She struggled to get out. Her eyes told me she was lying, but her words—her words made me think differently. Releasing her, I shoved from the wall, not even a backward glance going her way. I needed to forget about her. About the brown-eyed girl who caused me to live in hell.

"Wait... What's your name?" The girl called out running after me. Did she have a fucking death wish? I stopped dead in my tracks turning around to face her.

She stayed where she was standing, probably sensing if she came any closer, it would be the end of her life.

"No."

"What do you mean no?" Her voice held confusion.

"Killer."

"Killer? That's not a name."

"You're right, it's a job. A thing." I took a step forward, and then another, eventually coming face to face with her. She had balls of steel. I could rip her apart right here, right now.

"A thing?" She was questioning every word that came out of my mouth. Aside from the anger and rage I was feeling, I was slightly amused by her reaction.

"It's what I am. A killer, and it is what you will be if you don't walk away from me right now," I whispered for her ears only.

"A killer?"

"No—killed." A shudder worked its way through her body as she looked at me as if I were fucking crazy. I couldn't blame her, but the truth was—I *was* crazy. I was so fucking crazy it wasn't even funny.

"You can't just kill people," she kind of said to herself. I laughed... my body shaking with humor. Did one of the guys set her up to this? To see if I could handle not losing my temper out in public? If so, they were about to make some money.

"I can. I will. Not only that, but I do. Now run

along, sweetie." I narrowed my eyes at her, my eyes growing dark with a warning. It would be the last one she got.

I watched her body sway with fear as she took a step back. Her fists were clenched, and there was a burning anger right under the surface of her emotions. She wanted to lash out at me. To scream. Oh, I could make her scream.

"Maggie, is this guy fucking with you?" A blonde walked up to her hooking their arms together. I looked at her sideways. She had a disgusted look on her face as if I would approach her friend.

"No. No. We were just done talking," the woman who now had a name said. Maggie. I racked my brain for a memory, anything that could connect me with this person. She said she recognized me, but she didn't say from where.

"All right, then. Beat it, dude." The blonde pushed her friend back as if I were going to attack her. I sneered, on the verge of ripping into this bitch.

"Why don't you go back to wherever it was you came from?"

The blonde's mouth had hung open for a moment before she snapped it closed, her eyes turning dark.

"I don't know who the fuck you think you are, but—" The bitch stepped forward causing my blood to sing. I almost wanted to get my hands on her just to see what kind of fucked up shit I would do.

"Kandace, enough..." Maggie butted in,

interrupting her. I glanced at the blonde, and then back to Maggie again.

"No, this fucker doesn't talk to women like that," she said to Maggie before directing her attention back to me. "Did your Momma not raise you with manners, asshole?"

"Kandace, it's fine." Maggie stepped in front of her, shielding her body from mine. As if removing me from her sight would get her to calm down. Maggie had balls, but at least with hers came a dose of common sense. The blonde was just fucking dumb.

"No, it's not, men don't talk to women like that. It's the twenty-first century, asswipe," the blonde yelled directly at me, her eyes narrowing in anger. Maggie was holding her arms back as she tried to push through her.

"Is it? I couldn't tell. You're complaining about me not respecting you or your friend, yet do you see what you're wearing?" Nothing she could say to me would penetrate the ice covered tundra called my emotions.

"Did he just call me a slut?" the girl asked her friend, astonished. I was done with this shit show. Instead of responding, I turned around and walked back toward the table. What happened next, I never saw coming.

"Hey, asshole." I heard the voice of the Kandace girl behind me and whirled around to face her. Her fist was raised and coming toward my face. The impact of her knuckles touching my skin didn't hurt. There was no pain, only anger and rage that she had been dumb enough to think she could touch me.

I didn't take notice of the prying eyes around us or that Maggie had grabbed her friend and pulled her away from me. Instead, all I saw was fire and hate. I was fueled and ready to go.

My hand shot out, gripping Maggie by the throat. If she wanted to take her friends place, then so be it. "You should have let me walk away the first time. You dragged your friend into our little mess and now you want to take her place. Huh? Is that it? You can't save everybody. It's time someone taught you that."

My fingers dug into her delicate skin. I could feel the blood pumping through her veins and the screaming of bystanders as I gripped her tighter.

"Killer." My name was being called, but I wasn't releasing the girl. No way in fucking hell. I was going to finish this.

"Let her go." Jaxon's voice entered my ears, but I didn't care. I just squeezed harder. A pain deep in my chest formed. It radiated down my arms and into my hands. I could hear her gasps for breath and see the flutter of her eyelashes as they closed. I could feel the slowing of the blood in her veins as her body began to shut down.

"People are watching, Killer." Jaxon's warning reminded me of the pain I could endure again. My hold on her went slack as I brought her into my body. She was breathing, barely, but she was. The crowd around us was watching intently to see my next move, to see if I would slaughter her.

I could practically hear their whispers.

"What have you done?" The blonde screamed, tears forming in her eyes. Why was she sad? She was the one who had done this.

"Give me the girl," Jaxon ordered. So I did. I released my hand from her throat and gave her to him. Something in my chest was giving way to the person that I was. I could feel a fracturing of my coldness falling away.

Why?

Pain spilled through my head forcing another memory through.

"You were a good person, Diesel. You deserved the best in life. I know I never told you this... that I waited until it was too late, but I love you."

No! No! She couldn't love me. Who was Diesel? Why couldn't I remember who I was?

six

MAGGIE

MY FEET CARRIED me down the hallway in a rush. I was tired of being terrorized by these people. Those who called themselves my friends while talking behind my back, and those who never went out of their way to care about the girl who was being bullied.

"Maggie's a fatty..." They taunted. The tears escaped my eyes without warning as I pounded down the hallway. I could hear their laughter and footsteps following me.

"Why're you running, Maggie? Are you trying to lose some weight?" Blake, who was Roger's best friend, yelled down the hall.

You're not fat, Maggie. These people are just fucking stupid. I had to tell myself that over and over again. Yet, I was running. I was running from the bullies while telling myself that none of it were true. Why was that?

"Are you crying yet?" Blake's voice entered my mind. It was cold, and it was directly behind me. As I turned around, I caught a glimpse of the steel like anger in his eyes. I had never done anything to him. I had hardly ever spoken a word to him.

"Just leave me alone," I gasped out. My chest was filled to the brim with sadness. The agony of it all weighed heavily upon me.

"Leave you alone?" He smirked. "What's the fun in that?"

His steps grew closer and closer until he was a foot away. I squeezed my eyes shut, holding them closed. I could make them go away. I could make all the hate and sadness in the world go away.

"Open your eyes, fatty. I have a surprise for you." I could make it stop. I could make the pain go away.

"OPEN. YOUR. EYES," he screamed in my face. I could feel his saliva on my cheek, but I didn't move so much as an inch. I wouldn't give him that satisfaction. I could feel his rage, yet I still kept my eyes closed.

"You little fucking bitch." His hand came up to my face, and I could feel the rush of air as the sting of his fist fell upon my face. More tears escape my eyes, but I didn't say anything. I didn't even murmur in pain. On the inside, I was screaming, begging him to leave me alone.

"Don't touch her." Diesel's voice met my ears. My eyes popped open, and I looked up. The look on

his face said he had seen the whole thing.

"Or what, cripple?" Blake goaded him. I was used to being the one who stuck up for him. It was always me carrying the weight of helping him. He didn't deserve to be treated like this. Neither did I, but that's what I got for being there for him.

"You think I'm crippled? You think I can't help myself?" Every step Diesel took and every word from his mouth came with a purpose.

"I don't think..." Blake snorted. "I know." Those were the last words that came from his mouth. I watched as Diesel's fist raised over and over again until he made sure the kid was left in a puddle of his own blood.

Classes had been dismissed an hour ago, and I knew if this had taken place during school hours, we all would be in trouble. However, the bullying never took place during the day. It was always away from prying eyes.

Blake laid on the floor, his body curled in on itself. I wanted to stop Diesel, yet there was a part of me that didn't want to. I knew I would though, just because I would never allow him to turn into them.

"Diesel." My saying of his name brought his mind back to the present as he looked at me with deep concern. His eyes glided over my tear-streaked face.

"Come with me," he ordered wiping Blake's blood off on his blue jeans. I was hesitant to follow him. Never had he actually asked me to follow him somewhere. Usually, I was doing the following all

on my own.

"Maggie," he said my name sternly, turning around to me. I was still standing where I had been the entire time. My muscles told me not to move, but the look in Diesel's eyes told me I needed to.

Forcing myself forward, I walked over Blake's still breathing form on the tiled floor and closer to Diesel. Once I was close enough that he assumed I was following, he headed toward the AG room.

When he turned into the classroom, and up the steps to the second floor that was never used, my body told me no. Don't follow. I had never been scared of Diesel. To me, he was a man who was on the verge of death with every breath that passed his lips. The things he had to endure in his life when he should've been making happy memories hurt my soul.

"Come on," he ordered, breaking me from my thoughts. Placing one foot in front of the other like a scared puppy, I walked up the stairs. The place smelled of books and dust. I watched him walk over to a far corner of the room where a big window overlooked the greenhouse on the other side.

"Didn't I tell you more than once you couldn't save everybody...?" It was as if he were whispering.

"I wasn't trying to save anyone. I just wanted him to leave me alone," I almost cried out. I wanted him to understand, to listen.

"You were, and you have been this whole

time." He whirled around so fast, I felt like I was going to be sick. My body quivered with built up emotions.

"I did nothing wrong," I yelled my voice growing weak. He crossed the room in what seemed like less than a second coming face to face with me. He reached his hand up, and on instinct, I flinched away. Not because I thought he would hurt me, but because it just had become a habit.

"You're so right, Maggie. You haven't done anything wrong. You have been the kindest individual you could be, and I understand that now. What you don't get is when I told you to stop..." his words stopped as his eyes dropped down to the spot where Blake's hand had touched me, "...to stop sticking up for me—you caring has brought all this on you."

His voice was soft, caring, and I wanted to press into his touch as his fingers gently ran across the slap on my cheek.

"I don't care. It was the right thing." The words didn't sting quite as bad as the reality of what they meant. I had been doing the right thing. I had been sticking up for Diesel because no one else would. Even if we were both damaged from the outcome of it all, I would rather have us both here than an early death for him.

"In reality, it isn't. You don't deserve to be called names." His breath could be felt against my own lips, and as I lifted my eyes up to his, I almost gasped. In those eyes, I saw a flicker of something that I had never seen in all the years I had known

PROJECT: k i l l e r

him. Love.

"It's not the names that hurt, Diesel. It's the physical things that hurt. I can wipe away the hurtful comments like a chalkboard, but I can't undo the physical. I can't make my mind forget what a slap feels like." A tear escaped my eye, sliding down my cheek. Diesel's thumb stopped it, pressing softly against my skin.

"You won't ever have to... I'll help you forget." His lips pressed against mine feather soft, the connection causing goose bumps to develop on my skin. His hand sunk into my hair softly as if he wanted to breathe life back into me. Was he afraid the others would shut out the goodness that was inside of me?

When he pulled away from me, my mind was spinning and my cheeks were flushed. Long gone was the very thought of pain. Now it was replaced with something else. He pressed our foreheads together and stared deeply into my eyes.

"I won't let them hurt you anymore. I won't let them break you, beat you, or make you weak. You didn't listen to my warnings. You didn't stay out of it. None of that matters though—all that matters now is that they stop hurting you. You were there for me, even when I didn't need you. Want you. I will be here for you."

"What's her name?" I could hear someone ask but couldn't answer. My throat ached as if someone had shoved a baseball bat down it.

"No idea. I never asked Killer, and at this point and time, I don't feel like going back in there to do so." The voice speaking was deep and robust. My body felt weak as I tried to move around in the arms of the person carrying me.

"Fuck. She's waking up. Let's get her to a room." I wanted to grunt, doing anything I could to let them know I was still here. I had no idea where I was or what was happening.

I hear the clicking of a door opening and my body being placed on soft sheets. I willed my eyes to open, but they wouldn't. It felt as if cinderblocks were laid upon them.

"We need to go get Greg," one of the voices said. Who was Greg? Were these people going to hurt me?

I heard the click of the door closing as whoever was in the room left. It was then I focused on getting my eyes to open. Think happy thoughts, I told myself—when in reality all I could see was the darkness in the man's eyes that I had loved. I knew it was him. Not just by looks, because he looked very different than he used to, but in my body, my soul. I felt a pull. Kind of like love at first sight, but more so along the lines of seeing an old friend after not seeing them for years. You just know.

As I focused on Diesel, who was now going by Killer, my eyes popped open. My throat throbbed, and as I tried to lift a hand up to my throat, I realized I was unable to do so. Was I paralyzed?

I tried wiggling one of my toes, and it worked. What the fuck was wrong with me? Panic seized me as I looked around the room. It was simple. A bed I was laying on the corner. A dresser with a TV in front of me. A closet to the right, and a door that lead to what I would assume was a bathroom.

It was personal living quarters, but why? Which led me again to the question of, where was I? My eyes swiveled around the room. No windows, no escape route.

I could hear voices approaching and forced my eyes closed not wanting them to think I was awake yet. What if these people wanted to kill me? After all, what was it Diesel was supposed to be? *Dead.* I had gone to his funeral. I had wept at his casket and clasped his hand in my own. Yet he was alive. Breathing, seething in rage. He had almost killed me.

Not only that, but it was completely obvious he hadn't a clue who I was. If he had, he wouldn't have ever laid a hand on me. The man I knew, and the man who he was now, were two very different people.

"What the fuck happened out there? I told you guys to lay low. Now you got people questioning us," a voice raged just outside the door. I forced myself to stay unmoving, which wasn't an easy feat when all I wanted to do was to run from wherever I was.

"Killer. He went off the rails. He's been in the training facility since we got back. I think this is someone from his past."

The person speaking couldn't have been any more correct. I wasn't just someone from his past, though.

"Fuck, Christ. What did you use to dose her

up?"

"L1," the man responded. What the fuck was L1?

"Good. Let's hope it doesn't have any adverse effects on her," the man who I assumed was the leader said sounding relieved.

"Do you want us to do some background work on her? I'm not sure she can ever leave this place. People in the club honestly thought Killer committed murder."

I could practically feel the anger and confusion filling the room. They weren't alone in their emotions. I wanted answers, too.

"Full background. Find out where she lives, placement of work, and any other information that would be helpful. She has free will to the entire building. She isn't to leave under any circumstances and let Killer know he isn't to have contact with her."

The man sounded disappointed as if he had expected more from Killer. I almost couldn't blame him. At that moment when he had his hands around my throat, I saw a lost man, a man who had so much hate and anger built up. He wanted to unleash fury on anyone who made him feel something he didn't want to feel.

Maybe that's what I did—made him remember.

"Yes, sir. I will let him know." That was the last voice I would hear for hours. No one would come to check on me or make sure I was still breathing. I would lie in that bed until whatever it was they had shot me up with wore off.

Eventually, I did. My toes wiggled, which led to the feelings in my legs coming to life. As I progressed, I attempted to stand, only to fall back on the bed at a strange angle. My body ached in a strange way as the drugs continued to wear off.

"Help." I tried to say, but nothing escaped my lips. My mouth felt as if it were filled to the top with cotton not allowing a sound to escape.

Without a way to move, and no voice to call for help, I used my legs to roll myself over onto my side. It was there I fell into a fitful sleep praying I could bring myself to be the one thing that could save Killer.

seven

KILLER

MY FISTS CONTINUED to beat against the punching bag. The sound of skin breaking filled the air. Blood seeped from open wounds on my knuckles, but I felt no pain. There were no feelings of hurt. Just gleefulness filling my blood with a high unlike any other.

Was it my fault that woman almost died? I had almost blown the cover of my people. I had almost lost us the power of freedom—and for what? For anger issues, for hate toward some little bitch.

I heaved a breath into my lungs and then another. My fists pounded into the bag harder, each hit fueling the fire inside of me. My muscles burned for a break. Memories invaded my mind.

"Thank you, Diesel."

FUCK!! I stepped away from the punching bag,

grasping the hair at my scalp painfully.

Who was Diesel?

She wore a red dress today. Her hair was in soft curls, and her body reminded me of a dancer's.

"Stop!" I cried out. I didn't want the memories anymore. I didn't care about who I was in the past or what meant something to me or not. I didn't know that person. I wasn't that person anymore. Those memories shouldn't have meant anything to me because I wasn't him.

"Killer," Gauge called my name, but I couldn't bear to listen to him. He believed in me. He thought my life would be easier if I embraced the memories. He was wrong.

"Killer. Listen to me." He tried to reach out to me again, but his efforts were worthless. I felt like I was drowning in water at the bottom of a pool. His voice was muffled, and as I looked up at him, all I saw was a blurry image. With fists clenched, I squeezed my head, pounding on the sides of it to knock some sense into myself. This had to stop. I was going crazy.

"When I see your pain and you hurt, it makes me want to try. It makes me want to live to see another day. You're my reason to breathe."

"NO!" I bellowed out again. She wasn't my reason to breathe—she was nothing. Whoever she was, she was nothing.

"Killer, stop, or I'm going to have to give you some L1." The mere comment of a drug once used on me pulled me from my mind. How dare he use a drug on me that was supposed to be banned.

"L1, really? You would use the one weapon they used on us all the time. You know what it was like to be in that facility, Gauge. To have your memories wiped. To have been given a number instead of a name. All I knew was that I had cancer, I died, and now I'm here. How could you threaten me with that?" I screamed. I was losing my shit. I was completely lost and for what reason? I had no answers, no one to turn to. Even if I could turn to someone, the very people who knew the answers I wanted to know would do anything they could to keep it under lock and key.

"Calm down. Deep breaths dude," Gauge said calmly. I listened to his voice, forcing each breath into my chest slowly.

Hitting the floor with a thud, I crawled into a ball. I couldn't see myself as a man at this moment. I wasn't acting like a man. I was broken, fractured straight down the middle.

"Someone get the stretcher. I think he's going into remission." I could hear Gauge yelling for help, but my eyes glazed over. My veins felt like they were filling with steel, like I was capable of any and all destruction.

Pain. Hate. Anger. Rage.

"Hurry, he's fading fast..." Gauge's voice was still there, but underneath it all, was something else. A tiny spark in the back of my mind. I held the match to ignite it, and I wanted it to catch on fire. I wanted to destroy. Set my memories ablaze and never have them again.

"We're losing him..."

Oh, they didn't have a fucking clue. Losing me would have meant they would've had to have actually had me at one point in time. We all knew that wasn't true.

"Get the gun ready," a man said above me. He was big, but I was bigger. I could snap his neck. I could take him out of his pathetic misery. A smile formed on my lips. They had no idea the monster that was about to be unleashed on them.

I felt the prick of a needle entering my arm but didn't care. There was nothing they could do once the Killer came out to play.

"Everyone stand the fuck back until it kicks in, and then we'll take him into medical housing for a while." I wanted to laugh at his pathetic attempts at warning the others. If anyone died today, it would be their fault. Blood may stain my hands, but it was their fault I had lashed out.

"You cannot stop me. Nothing can stop me," I growled.

"Come back to me. You can't leave me here. God, you can't take him. You can't." I could hear her cries and feel her tears against my skin. It wasn't real... It's not real.

"Shoot him again," someone yelled. Another prick to my arm, which caused me to fill to the brim with rage, lashing out even more. The steel shot through my veins moving my muscles and causing my body to bow off the floor. My head was hazy and the room spun as the walls began to close in on me. Those who seemed far away were now right on top of me, their faces masked in hate.

"I'll kill you all," I screamed.

"Come back to me. You can't leave me here. God, you can't take him. You can't."

"Stop fighting it, Killer." I shook my head hysterically. Her words echoed inside of my mind... It was like a prayer to my heart.

"Come back to me. You can't leave me here. God, you can't take him. You can't."

I clung to her words. As my body settled into a deep darkness, the light before my eyes dulling like a candle that had been burnt out. The light dimmed until eventually... it was gone.

I was gone.

Sweat trickled down my spine as the coldness of the chains pressed against my wrists, biting into my skin. I could feel the blood seeping out of the wounds the metal had caused from me being suspended in the air by my arms. My body sagged, weariness threatened to take me, and yet he kept on with his torture.

Whip. Another lash to my torso as a sinister smile spread across my face. The pain left behind by the whip was nothing compared to the fury that was threatening to escape.

"You can whip me all you want. I won't obey on my own accord," I said, bitterness in every word I spoke.

"You will... or we get the L1. Oh, and me whipping you is more fun for me than a technique used to get you to obey." The cockiness in his words made me manic. I could feel the madness running through my veins as I closed my eyes,

gritted my teeth, and took a deep breath.

"Fun for you? Well, now it's time for me to have a little 'fun' of my own." Before he registered what I had said, I mustered up all the strength I had left in me and grabbed the chains, winding the metal around my hands. This movement lifted me higher up, and when I had a good grip, I yanked as hard as I could. With a loud snap, the chains instantly broke from the lock that was cemented into the ceiling as my blood pumped through me in a frenzy. The sound of my feet hitting the ground echoed throughout the cold, white room.

Standing up, I took a step closer. A step closer to my victim. Chaos swirled around in my head as the broken chains dragged behind my bloodied and battered body. No longer was there humor in his eyes. No, there was fear, fear that made me happy, crazy with a need to destroy. I watched as he brought the whip up, his hand trembling as he lashed it at me, the thin leather wrapping around my wrist as it cut into my skin. I wanted to laugh. Was this his way of stopping me from hurting him? From ripping his still-beating heart out of his chest?

With precise precision, I grabbed the whip that stood between my tormentor and me. I pulled with all my might watching as he tried to resist me, to fight back against my strength. As if he could hide from the anger that he had stirred inside of me. The friction of my skin against the leather caused the whip to slice my palms wide open. I could feel the blood dripping from the wounds, but my mind *was on the man before me. A demented smile formed on my face as he fell to the ground landing on his knees. With a flick of my wrist, I was wrapping the whip around his neck while I wiped the blood from my torso. The blood he had caused me to bleed, I smeared across his face.*

"Don't... don't kill me. I didn't want... they made me do everything to you." His words came out in a rush as I listened to him beg and plead for his life.

"It's a little late for that." There was no mercy in my voice, no remorse for the things I was about to do to him. I was a killer.

Those were the last words I had said to him before I ripped him to shreds, piece by piece. The last words before I came down from my high of vengeance. From my high of retribution. Of the need to feel his blood coating my hands in return for him making me bleed.

"11." The voice crackled through the speaker that was located by my door of captivity.

"11. Congratulations. You learned the lesson in today's training. Kill for revenge."

***

When I awoke, my head throbbed. I wasn't sure what was up or down. The blankets before me weren't my own. The bed not my own, yet I was here. In this bed. There were no restraints, and as I looked at my arms for injection marks to see if it was all a nightmare, I realized I truly had gone off the rails.

"How are you feeling?" Gauge asked me. My gaze swung to him. He was standing in the doorjamb staring at me with a grave look of disappointment. Somewhere inside of me, I knew the way he was looking at me should've mattered, that me hurting him and my brothers should've of bothered me. Yet it didn't.

"Like I got hit by a fucking truck. "

"It's the L1." One letter plus one number was the result of me losing control over my own body. He knew I hated that drug, yet he doped me up on it anyway.

"We didn't have an option. You ended up almost killing a woman, who we had to bring in, and then you just totally lost it. We had to do what we could to calm you down. You were manic, and we didn't know what you would do."

I didn't want to blame Gauge for having to shoot me up. I don't remember what happened, but I'm certain I was too far gone in an uncontrollable state if he had to put me down. I rubbed a hand down my face. Sweat clung to my hair and tension filled my belly. *The woman.* I remembered her and her stupid fucking friend.

"I don't blame you, Gauge. You did what you had to do." I sighed. I didn't want to deal with the emotions swirling around in my head, the memories festering in my brain, never leaving. With each old and new memory, I knew just as much as I did from the last. *Nothing.*

"I didn't think you would blame me." He

sounded like he knew me, like he understood how I would feel when I woke up. For some reason, it didn't settle with me. I didn't want to be close to anyone.

"Now, I did some talking with Jaxon. He told me about your behavior at the bar and with the woman. At first, I wanted her as far away from you as we could get her, but now we think it would be a good idea for you to talk to her."

Talk to her? I was off the bed and pacing the floor in a second flat. Just like the fire burning in my veins at the simple thought of talking to her again.

"Talk to her?" I laughed like the evil fucking man I was. "I almost killed her. More than likely, I'll do it again. I have a short temper, and I don't do talking. Fucking. I can do that. Fighting. Beating the oblivion out of someone. Perfect... but talking, no fucking way." I growled at Gauge.

The look on his face said he didn't give a shit what I said, and chances were, he didn't. He would do whatever he saw fit for our people. There was no official name for those who had been rescued or escaped, but Jaxon and I could only describe it as a colony.

Society knew of us, the super-men. The people who helped protect others. At least that was what the corporation made them think we were made for.

They turned a blind eye to what the company did to us thinking it was for the better good of the people. If one person had to die for others to live, they didn't see a problem with it. After all, most of us were going to die anyway.

"You will, or you won't be allowed out of confinement." Gauge narrowed his eyes at me. I had never asked him about his time with the corporation. We never knew the name of the company and he never told us. Thinking about it now, it was for the better. Had we known, we probably would've ambushed it by now. There would be no need for a safe haven like this—like Gauge had created.

"You can't keep me in confinement. I'll go insane." I was losing it just thinking about it. My fists were clenched, my black t-shirt sticking to my chest. I felt like I was in a box already, and all he had done was mention it.

Gauge shook his head smiling. "Then I suppose you pick option number one?" I turned, shooting a dark look at him. Of course, he would feel smug about it. He had been bringing up talking since I got out. He wanted me to get in touch with my emotions. To learn to feel. Most of all, he wanted me to talk about them.

The memories.

He thought if I were more open to them, then I would understand them more.

"I don't want to fucking do this..." There was pain in my words. I was trapped with no way out. I hated Gauge for putting me in this position, but I hated the corporation even more for doing this to me.

I should've died.

"Number one it is," I growled slamming my body down onto the bed. I had to learn to overcome this shit, and Gauge knew it. His idea of doing so was taking it head on, but only time would tell if I could become more than just a man, genetically altered to kill.

eight

I COULD HARDLY answer the questions Gauge was shooting at me. The second I gave him the answer to one question, he was asking another.

They still hadn't told me where I was or why I was still being kept here. It had been two days, two days of being held up in that room. There were no windows, no breeze, or sun. The rooms were nice, but they weren't the same as having my own freedom. They brought me meals, made sure I had fresh towels, and Gauge had even sent someone to my place to grab some of my things, but every visit always lead to the inevitable. The questions. The accusing looks. I wondered if I would ever be able to leave...

Then again, after having just found Diesel, I

wasn't sure I wanted to leave. Unless he was leaving with me.

"I told you everything already," I said for the third time or maybe it was the fourth. I couldn't remember. All the questions started to blur into one. My voice was still very much hoarse and talking only made it worse.

"You work for PGI Corporation, yet you don't know what they do there besides find cures for things such as cancer and other diseases?" Something in what he said caused me to tilt my head sideways at him. Either he didn't believe me or he liked listening to me talk.

"That is exactly what I told you, what I have been telling you, and what I will continue to tell you. The company comes up with miracle drugs and shit. I don't know what else they do. I've only been there six months. I was planning to work my way up into the curing sector." Gauge watched me intently as if he thought he could catch me in a lie. His eyebrows rose and then came back down as he digested what I had said.

"Until what?" he questioned in an accusing tone as if he had found a hole in something I had said. I shook my head in astonishment. What the fuck was he talking about?

"What do you mean until what?" I ran a hand through my hair, fully intent on ripping it out. I didn't understand what I had done wrong, and all his questions made me nervous. My stomach rolled in fear, and tension filled my muscles. Of course, I wanted to run. I didn't understand what it was that

I was doing wrong.

"I mean, you made it sound like there was going to be an 'until' or a 'but' somewhere in your sentence." He was definitely trying to find me in a lie. I wanted to ignore him but couldn't because he was standing right in front of me. Instead, my mind automatically turned to my thoughts on Diesel. How he was still alive. How I had taken that shit job just to get closer to doing something for him. Now he was alive, and I felt like finding a cure was the last thing I needed to do. He didn't even know who I was or what it was that made us who we were.

"Until Diesel." I let the name roll off my tongue like I hadn't said or thought the name a million times over. As if it wasn't him who made my heart beat.

"Hmm...." Gauge scratched at his chin, allowing silence to fall between us before speaking again. "I want you to know you aren't going to be leaving this place for a while." He paused, a dark look showing in his green eyes. "And when you do end up leaving here, it will be to do a few things for us." It was as if he was warning me, but about what? What was their plan, and where did I fit into it.

A film of sweat formed on my hands, and I wiped them off on my jeans. My saliva felt like sludge sliding down my throat as I swallowed. I could do this. *Right?*

It was then I realized what he had said and anger shot through me like it never had.

"What do you mean I can't leave? I have a right to leave. I'm a human. I'm a US citizen. I have

Page | 93

rights, damn it." I tried to keep my voice strong, attempting to get my point across. Gauge pushed out of his chair away from the table only to lean on it. His body was pure muscle. His face a mask of anger.

"Well, your *rights* are now useless. Your *rights* are gone. The fact that you work for the very company that put these men here takes those rights away. You deserve nothing from us," he hissed. Long gone was the negotiating.

"I don't understand what you're trying to say." I stuttered over my words, confused as to what PGI had to do with me being held wherever it was they were holding me. Things were failing to line up correctly, and I was starting to wonder if they even have a legit reason to keep me here.

Anger zinged through the air. "Let me put this as easily as I can. The company you work for transformed young men into genetically altered beings." My breath stilled in my chest—it couldn't be true. It had to be a lie, a ploy to get me to stay here.

"They wiped their memories away, except for the ones they wanted them to remember. Trained some of them to be lethal killing machines, forcing them to kill day in and day out. Others were turned into lab rats. Injections were forced upon them. Some were used for genetic changing drugs while others were cures for cancer. Plain and simple, they were experimental monkeys. The cure for AIDS you hear so much about..." My eyes grew wide, and I couldn't help the hand that flew up to my mouth as he paused mid-sentence. It couldn't be—there was no way society had allowed such a thing to take place.

"Yeah, sweetie, your people forced that on my people. That drug didn't come about from just thin air. It was used on MY people. Processed until there was an exact cure for that disease."

Tears formed in my eyes. How could they do that? Immediately, I wondered if Roger knew. If that was what all his secrecy was about.

"It can't be…" The words escaped my lips. I was astonished. A tear slipped from my eye, trickling down my cheek. I watched Gauge's eyes follow my tear. There was no compassion in his eyes, and I understood why. It was true—everything he had said was true. My heart ached, and the contents in my stomach threatened to come up.

"It is. Your tears mean nothing to us. We aren't looking for sympathy or understanding. All we want is retribution. Which we will get in due time. For now, we will settle for what we can get. I will keep this tidbit of information between you and me as long as you do as I say." His voice held authority and caused shivers to run down my spine. Was I being blackmailed?

"What do you want me to do?" I asked hesitantly unsure if I wanted to agree to anything he had to say. Diesel was a lethal monster now, a man I no longer knew. A smile formed on his face, and I should've taken it as a warning.

"I want you to work with Killer." My jaw all but hit the floor. He wanted me to work with Killer.

Killer who was technically Diesel.

"I don't—"I didn't get a chance to finish what I was saying because Gauge cut off my words. The table before me went flying with one swipe of his hand. With brutal force, it hit the far wall with a loud thud, and then he was right in my face like a raging bull.

"You will do whatever the fuck I tell you to do. If that little secret doesn't help keep you in line, then the fact that I know who Killer is to you will," he seethed. My arms went slack falling to the sides of my body. My chest heaved with every breath. How had he figured that out? How had he discovered anything about my job, about whatever it was that PGI did?

"He—"I mumbled. "He tried to kill me. He wrapped his hands around my neck until I couldn't breathe. He isn't the same person I knew. He doesn't recognize me, and he doesn't care. He was going to kill me. I saw the look in his eyes." I sounded hysterical as I shook my head back and forth. I had once loved Diesel. But the man who almost forced the life out of me wasn't Diesel. He was a monster, one on a mission for death.

Gauge stopped my head from shaking with a hard grip to my chin causing me to come face to face with him. He was so close I could feel his breath on my face. Terror grew deep within me. He looked like he was about to shake me to death.

"It doesn't matter. We won't tell him who you are until his memories allow him to remember you. That's what you will be doing. You will be working through his emotions with him, his memories of the two of you. He won't hurt you. He has promised not to."

I wanted to snort. This man had a very trustworthy heart if he thought Killer wouldn't try to take my life again if he got the chance. He had almost killed me without cause—what would he do with a cause?

"Oh, yeah, because that is so believable. In fact, almost everything you're saying is hard to believe. Impossible even," I said straight into his face, unable to turn away from him. His grip on my chin tightened to an almost unbearable state.

"Once you get out there and you start interacting with Killer—once you hear all he has gone through, once you spend one night listening to his screams, you will know all I have said to you is true. It's only impossible to believe because you haven't seen it yet." His voice was right next to my ear, his words being forced into my mind causing me to think, making me feel.

As soon as he was done talking, he released me. I wanted to reach up and rub away the pain that had formed in my jaw, but I wouldn't give him the satisfaction.

"Report to the arena in ten minutes time. Be prepared to see him. He knows you'll be there." Those had been Gauge's final words to me before he left what I now considered to be the interrogation room with a slam of the door.

The sound vibrating throughout the room shook me to the core. Diesel was alive. He was

Killer. His humanity completely gone as he cared for no one but himself, and the others who were like him, but... he was alive. That was one constant in all those things, one thing that mattered above all.

I wanted to cry... to hate him for not knowing that it was me. After all this time, after all my praying, and dreams of hoping he was alive...

"I wish I was dead..."

I recall the moment he said those words to me. It was days before he actually died. Well, died a fake death. None of this made much sense to me. What I did know was when I leave this place, if what Gauge had said was true, I would do anything and everything I could to bring PGI to its knees.

Ten minutes passed faster than I thought it would. I took a deep breath as I stood. I was scared. Beyond scared. Yet butterflies filled my stomach. I had a need to see Killer even if it wasn't meant to be. Even if he didn't want to see me.

I walked the hallway, keeping my eyes trained on the white tiles lining the floor. The walls were painted an off-white color, which lead me to believe they painted them that color to not make it look overly clean.

I could hear the pounding of fists against a punching bag. Laughter and voices filled my ears. I wondered if they have other women here. The way Gauge talked made it sound like PGI only used men as experimental monkeys.

I stopped just shy of two doors that reminded me of a high school gymnasium's entrance. There was a small piece of glass cut out that allowed me to peek through and look inside. On the other side of the doors was literally the biggest sports complex I had ever seen in my life. A boxing ring was centered in the middle of the room. There were mats everywhere you looked. Doors that lead to locker rooms. Men of all shapes, sizes, and ethnic colors were inside working off whatever aggression they had.

A throat cleared behind me, causing me to turn around with a shriek.

"You going in, sweetheart?" My cheeks grew red in embarrassment. I had been caught gawking. The man before me stared hard, his gray eyes darkening with every second that passed.

"Uhh..." was all I said, all I was able to get out. He was shirtless, his abs and, well, everything else on display. He gave me a dimpled grin. As he smelled the air, his nostrils flared. Then, without warning, he pushed the door behind me open drawing attention to us.

I guessed it was do or die. Turning around, I walked into the arena. Attention turned to me, and I could hear my heartbeat in my ears. Eyes drifted upward as I stepped further into the room.

"Welcome, Maggie," the man who had forced me to come in said. I gave him a small smile. "Oh, and just in case you need something, my name is Jaxon."

My stomach clenched when he turned to face me, throwing a wink my way before walking away, heading into the locker rooms.

"Maggie." I could hear my name being called by

Gauge, and I almost didn't want to recognize him. After all, with him came Killer. The man I had once loved. Hell, who was I kidding? The man I still *did* love. My knees shook, my hands were sweating, and something inside of me said I needed to get moving.

With my face casted down toward the floor, I crossed the mats, trying to keep out of the way of those who seemed to be doing something. Once I was directly in front of them, my eyes lifted to a pair of blue eyes that had caused so many different feelings to form within me. I had lived and loved through those eyes. They were a portal to our past. A pair I knew all too well. Or used to know at the very least.

How I looked at him without feeling fear, I didn't know. All I knew was I wanted to wrap my arms around him and beg him to remember me, to force him to see the love inside of me, the feelings I had for him. Yet even though I knew he wouldn't, and even when he did... I didn't know if he would look at me the same after all of this.

I didn't know if I could pull the Killer out of him without being killed myself.

nine

KILLER

SHE LOOKED AT me like she was sorry, like I was the beaten down dog—as if I wanted her fucking sympathy or something.

"Maggie. Killer. Killer. Maggie." Gauge introduced us even though he didn't need to. I had already had my hands wrapped around her neck. I was positive we were past introductions.

I tipped my chin up acknowledging her all while watching the way her facial expressions changed. They went from shocked to sad and then to neutral as if to hide her real feelings. I wasn't sure I wanted to talk to her—to bring up my past. The looks that shadowed her face told me I was going to get emotions I wasn't comfortable with.

Calm.

No words were said by either of us, which

caused the tension to pull taut like a rubber band. Her eyes bled into mine. The brown was a softness that reminded me of coffee and chocolate. Her hair was messy and had a small curl at the ends of it.

"Killer." As she said my name, I almost groaned. Her full lips had spewed questions I didn't want to answer just days ago. Now, with her lips saying my name, I was ready to cut the shit and do whatever I wanted with her. *Fuck her. Make her bleed.*

"Killer agreed to behave with you. Your first few sessions will be in here with the rest of the men just to make sure all is okay between the two of you. Then, once things die down a bit, you can have some alone time." Gauge talked to us as if we were children.

"That's fine with me," Maggie said. *Maggie.* As I rolled her name off my tongue a number of times in my mind, I realized I had heard that name before.

I cracked my knuckles watching her eyes grow wide. Was she scared of me? She should be. I was worse than any monster she had ever heard about.

Gauge shot me a warning look as he walked away leaving us with one another. The guys around the room stared for a short time watching to see what I would do next. To everyone here, I was the ticking time bomb. No one knew when a memory was going to hit me, or when I was going to go off the rails in a blaze of fury.

Maggie took a step back until she was against the far wall. From there she slid down it, sitting with her back against it. I followed suit, making sure there was distance between us. I didn't like people touching me. More than that, I needed distance between us. My mind was racing, and there was nothing stopping me from taking her now.

"Why did you try to kill me?" Maggie asked behind a shield of dark hair. Her question startled me, yet at the same time, it humored me. I wanted to laugh. That was her opening question? I suppose she deserved an answer.

"I didn't try to kill you. I tried to kill your friend. You got in the way. I was already too far gone to stop, so..." I trailed off. I didn't know what else to say.

"Then why did you stop?" She looked up at me this time, her own eyes holding heat that I hadn't seen before. Her body was small... Almost too small. She was wearing a light gray shirt and a pair of black jeans. Not what I remembered her wearing the last time I saw her, which only meant someone had gotten her some clean clothes from somewhere.

There was no saying what she looked like underneath it all. My body reacted to the thought though. My cock grew hard at the mere thought of stripping her bare and fucking her until she screamed—until her body withered beneath mine until she begged me to stop.

"I don't know..." I growled. I knew why I had stopped, but I wasn't going to tell her why. I didn't trust her. I never would. Trusting humans was one of the most senseless choices I, or any of the other guys in this room, had ever made. To trust was to put your life in someone else's hands. I had done that once before and look where it got me.

"Oh, I thought maybe it had something to do with a conscience or something." Her tone was all smartass as she smiled. When I didn't return the smile, it slipped from her face. Did she think this was a joke? I could feel my blood boiling with the need to feel the warmth from her blood covering my body. Coating me in slickness, covering all the memories that I wanted to leave me.

"Maggie..." I said her name as softly as I could, staring deeply into her eyes. I forced my hands to my sides afraid if I touched her, I would hurt her. "You need to be aware of something. No one in this room has a conscience. Every single person would gladly snap your neck. We don't care for humans. We don't care for those who watched idly as we suffered."

Emotions swarmed her and tears formed in her eyes. I wanted to howl. Tears. They were weakness leaving the body. They were proof of heartache, of pain—somethingI could no longer experience.

"I never did those things..." Her voice hitched, which showed further why this whole deal with Gauge wouldn't work. She was human, and I wasn't. Her emotions were real, her feelings real. My anger and madness would destroy her.

"It doesn't matter..." I leaned into her space causing her chest to rise and fall fast. The spike in her pulse showed fear... *Good*. "The fact that you bleed and are of flesh and bone as they are, and your mind works the same way—the fact that you probably knew and did nothing to help it..." I leaned in even closer, my nails digging into my hand painfully to remind me that touching her wasn't ideal.

Her chest heaved another breath, and I smiled. I was a sick fuck getting off on her sadness and fear. "If I knew, I wouldn't have let it happen..." she mumbled. I could feel the prying eyes of others on us.

"You would have because you're just like them. If you and your friend had left me alone, you wouldn't even be in this mess right now... You would be carrying on with your lives without a care in the world, uncaring of those who were being worked on like guinea fucking pigs."

Another tear fell from her eye. I wanted to reach out and smash the droplet. Make it nonexistent. In the same instant though, I wanted to lick it, to taste the saltiness that was she on my tongue.

"I'm truly sorry." She apologized as if she knew what she was saying sorry for, as if her apology would make up for all those who had suffered. She knew nothing, and I wanted to wipe the floor with her pathetic apology.

"Then prove it...." I growled, unaware of why I said that. What could she prove to me? She had nothing I wanted.

"How—" she stuttered. "How do you want me to prove it to you?" Her chin was held high and her eyes narrowed at me as if she knew what I was getting at.

"I can't tell you how to prove it. All I can tell you is you have put me through the ringer in the last forty-eight hours. You caused my mind to go crazy... If you had died..." I leaned into her body, taking in her scent. It filled my nostrils causing something in my mind to snap. "If you had died, it wouldn't have hurt me. It wouldn't have caused me any pain. I would've looked at you like I did the man who I had killed the night before. When I told you to leave me alone..."

Something happened inside my head. Pain radiated through me as I gripped at my scalp. The memory came out of nowhere, forcing the air from my lungs.

"I tried to make them stop..." Her voice was so broken. Shock and horror were written all over her face. There was nothing she could do that would change their behavior. They didn't understand why they hated her or me.

"Shhh, it's okay." I rubbed a hand through her hair and down her back. The things they had done to us both... I needed to learn to let go of my hate for them. I was close to meeting my maker, and I didn't want to take that to my grave.

"It's not okay. It's not okay because we're human, too. We have feelings..." Her tears seeped into my t-shirt as I took every fear she had away.

"I know, but we're better than they are. We're different."

When I opened my eyes, Maggie was hovering over me, her small hand on my arm, concern etched into every contour of her face.

"Are you okay?" she asked her voice meek and laced with fear. She had no clue. I wanted to sneer at her, to smack her hand away. I wanted to blame her for the memories, but I knew it wasn't her fault. Deep down under the blackness that was pumped into me laid a heart, a muscle I hadn't used in forever. I could feel the blood rushing to it. Every memory was bringing me that much closer to humanity.

"I'm fine," I muttered as I sat up. With every memory came a weakness. A weakness to give into what my body wanted. *To remember.* To me, it wasn't that easy. With the memories would come the past, and though I would never admit it vocally, I had a fear far greater than the memories. I had a fear of finding out who the girl was and then realizing she was no longer here, and slipping back into the person I was made to be.

The memories didn't haunt me. I wasn't angry because of them. I was angry for what they represented.

My past—my future.

ten

MAGGIE

His words hit me like a ton of bricks. I stared at him in awe. How could he be so mean, so hateful? *I would've looked at you like I did the man who I had killed the night before.* How could he think that killing someone was okay?

I wanted to reach out and grab him, to shake some sense into him. Now more than ever I wished the memories would come to the surface.

"Do you—" I paused watching his eyes grow darker. I was positive talking wasn't anything he wanted to do. When he looked at me, I saw two things in his eyes. He either felt rage for me or he wanted to fuck me, and I wouldn't allow that to happen. At least not in this place, and not while he was this person—this person I didn't know.

"Do I what?" he responded gruffly.

"Do you want to talk about it?" I knew something had hit him. The faraway look in his eyes gave it away. It was as if he was here, but his mind wasn't. He was reliving the past in great detail. For some reason, it made me want to know what parts of his memory were resurfacing. If they were parts of us... memories of things we used to do. Memories of what had happened between us.

"Talk about what?" he scoffed. His fists clenched and unclenched. Right off the bat, I had gathered what his triggers were. He didn't like being asked questions or talking about things that could trigger a feeling or an emotion.

Somewhere, somehow, I had gotten balls. I narrowed my eyes at him and crossed my arms over my chest. "Don't play dumb with me..." He smirked at my tone, his tongue darting out to wet his perfect bottom lip before speaking.

"Did you just threaten me?" He tilted his head sideways at me as he moved closer. My stomach filled with knots. Had I made the mistake of getting smart with him? Would he snap my neck right here, right now? Would anyone be able to get to me in time? The walls felt as if they were closing in on me.

"I just want you to talk about your feelings, the memories. I'm only doing what Gauge told me to do." I wanted to scream the words at him, to shine a light on him, and make him understand.

"What you don't get...." He leaned into me, his eyes glazed over and with no caring nature. Whatever the memory was, it had done nothing to bring him closer to humanity. His fist clenched as he brought his hand closer to my face. I could see the hugeness of it, the callousness of his rough skin in comparison to my own, and the desire in his eyes to reach out and grip me.

"What you don't get," he repeated, "is that I could very well snap your neck. I could kill you before a scream ever escaped those plump lips. I could cause you so much pain and agony you would wish for me to kill you. I could—" He paused again, unclenching his fist, and then clenching it slowly in front of my face. He was showing me what he could do with his hands... the damage he could cause.

It's a warning.

"I could destroy you with one flick of my wrist. I could bring your very existence to an end. You should feel very lucky to have even had the chance to breathe the same air as me." His voice was a growl that caused shivers to ripple across my skin.

"This isn't how this is going to work." I was annoyed. I was more than annoyed. I was pissed off. This man, the man I had spent years craving and mourning over, turned out to be an inhumane asshole. I felt nothing for him when he talked this way.

"Oh, but it is, you see, I don't have to do this. I had more than one option, and the way it's looking right now, option two sounds much better."

I bit my own lip stifling the remark I wanted to make. I didn't want to hurt him, but I couldn't allow him to keep treating me this way. His only way of hurting others was through fear, threats, and his words. Violence being his only form of communication.

"I think we're done for the day…" I murmured getting up from my sitting position. I didn't even look over to see what Killer would do. There was no reason for me to do so. Yet, as I stood, so did he.

I was taken back as I felt his hand dig into the soft flesh of my shoulder. He leaned into me and began to whisper. "You can't change me. They have been trying for months to get me to talk, to release my emotions. If you think you can do any better than them, you're just as naïve." With every word, I felt his fingers sink deeper and deeper into my flesh. I wanted to scream, to cry out in pain. But I didn't. I knew it was what he wanted. He wanted to feel my pain, to know I was afraid and cowering because of him.

Instead of doing either of those things, I buried the pain. I forced myself to look straight into his eyes and smile. It was that smile that would crumble him. It would bring him to his knees. He could say all he wanted how this was about the differences between the two of us, but in the end, it wasn't.

It was about him letting the memories come. He was afraid more than anything. The fear would eat him alive if he allowed it to do so.

With a shove that had me off kilter, he released me and made his way out of the arena like a bat out of hell.

He's scared.
He's afraid.
He just wants to be saved.

I told myself those things over and over again. As I walked down the hallway, as I ate my dinner, and as I sat on the bed they had provided me—and when I laid down that night and closed my eyes, it was images of him that haunted me. Memories surfaced and I was unable to push them away.

"Prom is tomorrow." I tried to sound nonchalant about it, but in reality, I wanted him to go with me. I knew he was sick and that it was risky being around everyone all at once. But I wanted him to be a high school student for once. To be able to dance under the stars, and to be happy.

"Mags, I won't go. It has nothing to do with you and you know it." That was my final time asking. If I asked anymore, he would lose it, and when that happened, we could go days without talking. Often he lost his temper. He never hurt me, but I had seen him hurt others. It scared me sometimes while other times it caused a zing to run through me.

"I know." I pouted. "I just wanted one ordinary night. One day where we could just go and be us."

"That will never happen..." He sounded like he didn't care, and it was times like this that I didn't like. When he was at the point of helplessness. When he was close to breaking.

"You're a pretender, Diesel. Of course, it will happen. It happens every day. So what? You're dying. Live for today, live for tomorrow, but never, I mean never try to say it won't happen. It's happening right now. You're breathing and that in

itself is normal." I didn't want to yell, but I couldn't hold back my anger.

I heard his deep inhale and exhale, and a shiver ran through me as he stood and walked over from his chair. He stopped right in front of me, his face full of aggression. When his hand came up to the side of my cheek, I shied away. He gripped my chin hard, pulling my face into his.

His breath blew softly across my cheeks. "I'm not a pretender. I'm a realist. Someone who only wants to protect you. Everything I do, Mags, I do for your own good." His lips pressed against my forehead hard as if he were trying to force his anger out in that one singular gesture.

"Protecting me would be going with me. It would be allowing us to have that one moment. It would be giving yourself a chance to let your guard down. To be free of everything. We could—" I didn't get to finish my sentence because his hand covered my mouth as he pushed me backward. The air escaped my lungs as I landed with a thud against the brick wall.

"If she comes tomorrow, I say we run her out of there in tears." I could hear one voice say but couldn't place who was saying it. Diesel moved us, pushing us further into the dark corner of the art room.

"I not only say that, but we rip her dress and get a little action. I have wanted to see her goods since freshman year." I knew that voice. I gasped against Diesel's hand in astonishment. Even in the darkness, I could see the 'I told you so' look

marring his face.

"I agree. Her tits are huge… Makes me wonder if they're even real," the other voice said as they moved over to the art supply room. I desperately wanted to speak out against them. To tell them just how wrong all the things they were saying and planning on doing were.

"Wherever Mrs. Jane said the supplies were, she was wrong. I can't find fucking shit in here," Roger said, wandering out of the supply room and back over to the table where Diesel and I had been sitting. He stared at it for a long time before glancing around the room. I knew he couldn't see us in the corner where there was no light. There was no way, yet with his prying eyes on us, I felt anything but safe.

"Is it me or does it look like someone was here?" Roger mocked, looking around the room again as if at any point in time someone would jump out and get him.

His friend, who I was finally able to see, was no other than Monty James. He plucked the paper Diesel had been working on right off the table.

"Name on the top says Diesel," Monty said to Roger before crumbling the piece of paper up. I shook in fear. I know it was wrong to be scared, to not stand up to them, but there was nothing that could be done.

"I'm going to go out there and get them to leave. Stay here, please." Diesel's voice pleaded with me as he whispered before pulling away from me. The warmth left my body as I watched him

step away and into the light.

"And there he is..." Roger sounded overjoyed. His happiness felt like a cold bucket of water being doused on me.

"Just leave. I don't know how many times I have to tell you that bullying me will get you nowhere. Who bullies someone who is dying? And when did it become okay to do this?" Diesel was trying to reason with him. He always tried, but it never did him any good. The look in Roger's eyes told me his words meant nothing.

"Leave? That would be doing something you want. No one ever believes you when you tell them what we do." Roger shrugged, growing closer to Diesel. I wanted to escape the dark corner and go save him, but I knew he would never forgive me.

"Go. Get away from me." I could feel the tension filling the room. The anger in Diesel's voice scared me, forcing me to stay frozen in place.

"Ahhh, are you the big bad wolf?" Both the boys laughed. Then Roger did something I never saw coming. He lunged at Diesel, his fist landing against Diesel's head. With the sickness already causing him weakness, he fell to the floor where they both jumped him.

I forced a hand over my mouth to stifle my screams as he faced me, his eyes telling me not to move. Minutes passed as the sound of bone hitting skin filled the room while blood dripped to the floor. Every crimson drop reminded me how much I truly hated these people.

Once they were done beating the shit out of

him, I scurried to the corner and held Diesel on the floor, allowing tears to fall from my eyes. I understood what he meant now. I was scared, too. I was so fucking scared, and when Diesel was gone, I wondered if I would be able to hold on. I was scared of a life without him more than I feared anything else.

eleven

KILLER

EVERY DAY FOR the past week was the same. Maggie and I would meet up every evening in the arena. We would argue going back and forth about my so-called shit behavior. She would try to invoke an emotion inside of me other than anger, but it never worked. I was either really fucking turned on around her or I was pissed off.

"How have your memories been?" she asked calmly as if she were analyzing me. She had gotten over her fear faster than I thought she would. Now she was more open and daring about the answers she wanted. I didn't want to answer her. She didn't need to know the memories had been coming at me from all angles every single night this past week, and how talking to her was just causing more of them to resurface.

"I have a question for you. Why the fuck did you sign up to do this?" I glared at her. There was more to the story than she was letting on. I knew she could at least go home and back to her normal life. Gauge had ways of keeping someone like her quiet. Her reason for being here wasn't that she had to be...

Her eyes refused to meet mine as they moved everywhere but to my face. Oh, fuck yes. There was definitely something going on below the surface.

"I didn't sign up for anything," she mumbled. Her cheeks warmed as if in embarrassment. What did she have to be embarrassed about?

"Then why are you still here?" I seethed, allowing a mask of anger to fall upon my face. I hated it when people felt as if they could lie to me. This was the problem with trusting people like her. You couldn't.

"First, it's not as if I really want to be here." She held up one finger signaling that there were a number of excuses coming my way. "Secondly, I can't leave..." She hid her face behind her long brown hair. I hated when people failed to make eye contact. Even more, I hated how she refused to meet my eyes. Sometimes, all it took was one look for me to understand.

"What else? There can't just be two fucking reasons as to why you can't leave..." I growled in frustration. Yammering about nothing did me no good. I didn't want to be around her, and I definitely didn't want to have to talk to her.

"Diesel, when did you—" Her voice stopped, her

eyes growing the size of saucers as her mind registered her mistake.

Diesel.

I had heard that name before. It was one often said in my dreams. The doe-eyed girl who was smiling, her face full of happiness, always said it.

"Who is he?" I asked urgently, now knowing Maggie was the key to finding out who Diesel was.

"Who is who?" she asked innocently. Did she think I was fucking stupid? Did she think I never cared to pay attention to the things said around me? I might have been quiet and anti-social, but I knew all that was said. In less than a second, I reached out and gripped her hard by the wrist.

"Do you think I'm stupid? Who is he?" My voice was mangled. I was on the verge of falling off the fucking cliff... into the deep darkness of void matter. I could feel my eyes growing black. I gripped at the table with my free hand. I needed something to hold me to the current world.

"I don't think you're stupid..." She stuttered over her words, fear overriding every other emotion in her body. I could practically see her running for the door, her fear rising, its smell so strong I could taste it.

"You do..." I growled. I was positive she was going to run—I mean, it would've been the logical thing to do. Instead, she looked at me, the fear dissipating into something else, something intense and raw. It wasn't love, but it wasn't hate. It was a balance between love and hate for herself. What I didn't understand was why?

"No... No, I... "She paused looking around carefully. "I don't think you're stupid, not in the least bit. I just think you ask questions you don't want the answers to." Her voice was soft and quiet.

My grip on the table slacked, but only for a second, before an image appeared in my mind. *A dress, it was soft and shiny. It sparkled in the light.*

"No..." I yelled my voice rising. A low whining formed in my head, and I could feel the current time slipping away as a past I didn't remember flooded my thoughts.

"Hey... what's the matter?" I watched as Maggie's face filled with panic. Her image blurred out... and before me formed a new one. One of the past. One that would hopefully tell me who Diesel was.

I kicked the rocks in the driveway of my parent's house. I hated them. The way they begged me to carry on with my life. Hell, I hated everyone. Everyone except Maggie. She was tolerable, or at least that's what I told myself. I wasn't man enough to admit I truly loved her. One would assume I did, considering everything I did for her. I looked up from the ground, my eyes gliding across the farmhouse as I tried to figure out if I should go to her or not.

I don't know how many times I told her not to go. That was one thing about Maggie that drew me to her. She was a rebel, living every moment for what it was worth, and she wasn't even the one dying.

Once I got my hands on her, her ass was going

to be grass. I could still feel the bruises against my ribs and the blood dripping from my nose. I wanted to be tough, even strong for her—but the truth was, I wasn't. I was weak and the cancer slowly destroying me from the inside out made me that way. It didn't matter though...

But it did, a little voice always said.

"Fuck it," I grumbled into the night air as I got into my car and headed into town. I gripped the steering wheel as if it were an extension of my own body. Like it could hold me to the ground for the time being.

The drive was short, even though it felt like an eternity, as I pulled into the parking lot. She had watched me get my ass handed to me, yet here she was playing this game with me. Was this a copout for me to admit my feelings to her? She knew we were both alone in this, and eventually, she would be left behind.

I gripped the wheel harder. Stupid, that's what she fucking was. Stupid and reckless, and... I couldn't force the words from my mouth, but it was right there on the tip of my tongue.

She was beautiful.

It didn't matter what way I tried to unravel it, everything would come back to her and me. There was no fighting something hell bent on happening. I opened my car door and slammed it shut with a push of my hand. My body still ached from the beating as I wormed my way through the parking lot. There were cars everywhere. It was no fucking wonder I never wanted to go to one of these functions. Too many people and too much wasted time.

I knew where they had one of the doors unlocked. So instead of heading for the entrance, I headed to the back and up the stairs to the second story greenhouse building that lead right into the school. I had taken Maggie up there once. It was my go-to place when I was feeling alone or needed time to myself.

I pulled my phone out and looked down at the text again. She hadn't sent it more than fifteen minutes ago. It was a standard and straight to the point Maggie text.

Mags: I don't like it here...

That was all it said. I read it over again for good measure before heading toward the doors that were located at the back of the gym. It was on that stroll to get Maggie that I heard a scream followed by male voices. I knew better than to be caught up in any more problems. I was beaten, I was bruised, and I had absolutely no reason to be playing the hero. Yet, something told me I needed to make sure it was all okay.

I headed in the direction of the scream and came to a standstill when my eyes landed on Roger leaning over Maggie on a table. She was pawing at one of his hands that were securing her arms while he wrapped his other hand around her mouth. Tears fell from her eyes... She thought this was the end for her. Her eyes connected with mine, and I could see the overwhelming surge of relief that formed inside her at seeing me.

j.l. beck

"Oh, did you come to join, Diesel?" Roger asked as he followed Maggie's line of sight. "I think there is room for two. I'll take the pussy, you take the ass... After all, I know how much you love it in the ass. So you should have no problem taking hers." He smirked, and I could no longer stop myself from reaching out and landing a blow against his cheek. He released Maggie to catch himself on one of the tables. How had the teachers allowed this to happen? They knew what they had done to Maggie. Roger and his little gang. I had told them. I had witnessed it. I had taken the pain for her on countless occasions. Yet somehow, someway, they had let this asshole get her all alone.*

"Who the fuck do you think you are?" I questioned as my fist landed against his face. Not giving him a chance to answer me, I hit him again as he tried to regain his balance. I didn't need him to answer me. I didn't want to know who he thought he was. He was dirt beneath my feet to me—and to Maggie.

He fell to the floor, tripping over his own feet. I could hear Maggie's muffled cries as she jumped off the table, tugging on her dress...

Maggie.

Maggie. I took a deep breath, my eyes popping open.

"Maggie," I said the name aloud just to make sure I had heard it correctly.

"I'm right here." Her voice was a faint whisper. My mind surged back to the present, but one word lingered there right in the void between the current and the past.

Maggie.

Was this Maggie the same Maggie from my past? And if so, why hadn't the name triggered something inside of me by now? Better yet, what was it Maggie knew that she wasn't telling me? If she were here, then she was pretending not to know me... and for some reason, it bothered me because if she were here on different terms, then that would put a target on her back.

A target I would be forced to take out.

twelve

MAGGIE

THE MEMORIES OF my past were a living, breathing nightmare. Watching Killer suffer in agony over the same past that haunted me hurt. The fact he couldn't remember the very things that we had gone through was another blow to my already broken heart.

All the bullying Roger had put us through, the hateful things said and done, the kisses, and the stolen looks... all the things I would've called my very reason for existing back then.

I triggered something in him when Diesel slipped past my lips instead of Killer. Another memory. I could see it spiraling out of control. He was free falling into open waters.

Once he remembered everything, would he even look at me the same way? After all, I had been working for the very man who beat him up numerous times. The same man who had almost taken my virtue.

I thought my life was hell before Diesel—it was worse once he was gone. Fear lived inside of me every minute of the day. I lived for those seconds when school ended and I could go home. Not that it was safe there either.

Eventually, Roger weaseled his way into every aspect of my life. With Diesel gone and no one to protect me, they took advantage of me. I could still remember my prayers for the pain to end.

"Maggie." I heard my name being called, and I moved from my slouched back position to a sitting position.

Three weeks had passed. Killer was much the same, minus the way he watched me. He would look at me differently, every so often staring when he didn't think I was paying attention.

"Gauge." I greeted him much as he greeted me. Cold and to the point. It was evident I wasn't here to make friends. Still, it would've been nice to have been greeted like a human.

"I need some kind of idea of how Killer is doing with his memories. I know he hasn't had any real outbursts or anything lately, but that doesn't mean something fucked up isn't going on inside his head." Gauge wanted reassurance as if I could offer it to him. I couldn't. There was no telling when Killer would snap next or who his next target was.

"Here's an idea—it's not working." I slammed my fist onto the table. "He doesn't care to talk about the past. He doesn't talk about the memories even though I'm in most of them. He doesn't even realize it's me who he's talking to. He's not getting any closer to remembering. If anything, he's getting closer to blowing up again." I heaved in a big breath. "And I think he hates this place."

It was the truth. He looked at everything, including this place as if it were a piece of shit.

Gauge paced the room for a short time as he scratched at his beard. Once I was sure he had walked a hole in the floor, he stopped and looked me straight in the eyes. He watched me the same way Killer did... except his stare was less calculating, less 'I want to snap your neck in twenty different ways.'

In a way, it was heartwarming, just because I was so used to being looked at as prey. This made me laugh a little bit. Diesel had never looked at me like Killer did. It was as if they were two different extensions of the same person.

"What if you leave this place?" I almost jumped for joy. Gauge must've seen my excitement because he rephrased what he said. "With Killer that is. Leave this place and go to the park or dinner. Do something normal that gives him a chance to open up his mind." He was set in stone about his idea while I was hesitant, to say the least.

"I have been missing for almost five weeks, Gauge. People are looking for me. I mean, at the very least, my best friend is. We shouldn't leave, as tempting as it is to me. If someone sees us—him or me, then it's over." I was sure of it, and the last thing I wanted was to be caught and smuggled to some island with an angry Killer. Diesel... yes. Killer, meh... I was on the fence with him.

Gauge eyed me before leaning over the small wooden table. My pulse jumped as he smelled the air around me.

"Are you aroused?" he questioned me. Did this fucker trip and hit his head somewhere? Me, aroused? By him? Yeah, I don't think so.

"No, I'm not, and I would greatly appreciate it if you would stop..." I paused, unsure of what it was that he was doing exactly.

"Sensing you. Reading you. You think we don't know shit about you. You think we don't have dirt on you to keep you here? If that's what you think, then run. We'll find you, and we'll drag you back here. You're Killer's emotional trigger. You can bring him back from the abyss. You knew him when he was human, and you're the only one who can help us. As far as people looking for you... guess you better stay out of their sight then." I wanted to laugh in his face. After five weeks of being here, my sense of humor had to be off. I couldn't tell what was funny and what wasn't.

"Do you hear yourself? You want me to help you, but yet you talk and treat me like this? What is it you have on me? What are you going to tell Killer to make him hate me more than he already does?" A dull ache formed in my chest at those very words. Oh, how I loathed them.

"You will do it because if you don't, we will tell him who it is you work for. I will tell every single person in this building, and they will rip you to shreds. You're the only revenge within grabbing distance. Could you handle your skin being ripped from your bones? Your screams echoing in your mind as they inflicted unimaginable pain on you?" The venom behind his words stung. I had never looked at myself as the enemy. I had never thought of what they could do. What they would do if they knew who I worked for.

"Why do you want him to remember so badly? How does it benefit you? Better yet, how do I know you won't kill me once he does remember?" I narrowed my eyes in questioning. His mouth snapped shut, his eyes growing angry. I had been here long enough without answers. They wanted me to do this and do that but refused to let me know the truth behind their desires.

"We want him sane. We want to be able to let him leave this place and know that he won't leave a slew of bodies in his wake. He kills people, Maggie. That's how he deals with the memories—and the pain. Remember that if you decide to cross him, or even me, all it takes is one word, one single word, and I will exploit you to the entire building, fucking up your very existence. Then we won't have to worry about what will happen to you when this is all over and done with because it will be taken care of."

He smiled a sickening smile, one that had my breakfast churning in my stomach. If Killer discovered who I was before I could get to PGI Corp, then there would be no point in trying to leave He loved the Maggie he knew just like I loved the Diesel I once knew. We both were two very different people now.

"I'm going to get the paperwork issued and let the guards know you're allowed to leave of your own free will—with Killer in tow at all times, though," Gauge warned me, shoving from the table and exiting the room.

I stayed seated not wanting to move from my chair. I needed to let what he had said sink in. Eventually, I found my bearings and headed for the door. I needed to go to Diesel and let him know there was a change in plans. I had just stood up when the door whipped open, almost coming off its hinges. Wood smacked against the brick wall as it cracked down the middle. My heart was beating against my chest as two black booted feet came into my line of sight. My eyes inched their way up his body, over the black cargo pants to his firm stomach, and over his well-defined chest covered in a black fitted t-shirt. His muscles bulged against the fabric as he crossed his arms in front of me, blocking my exit from the room. I was scared... but at the same time, I could taste the danger on my tongue as it swirled in the air.

My eyes landed on his almost black ones. He narrowed his eyes at me, walking into the room and into my space.

"You think I don't know what you're up to?" His voice was gruff.

"I'm up to nothing. I just want to know what was so urgent you had to break down the fucking door." My eyebrows shot up as I peered at the door. He took another step forward, and I watched the knuckles of his hands grow white. I could feel the energy of whatever it was that was making him angry around me. It rolled off him in waves, each one threatening to knock me down.

"I know something is going on..." He leaned into me, his nose almost touching mine. It was times like these when I lost the image of who Diesel truly was. His hand rose as he pressed a finger into the side of his head. "I can feel it in here. I can feel the crumbling of my mind. I can feel the memories resurfacing, and I think—" His voice cut off as he looked at me as if he were astounded by what he was about to say.

"I think I know you..." He narrowed his eyes taking in a deep breath of air. My chest constricted, sweat formed on my hands, and my stomach dropped. He couldn't know. He couldn't find out. Gauge had told me he would need the antidote to remember me or anything else from his past. The therapy was just a fluke to see if the memories would actually trigger him to come back to the present.

"I'm right, aren't I?" He didn't question me, it was more so a question to himself. I couldn't answer him. My throat felt dry, and the longer I stood there, the deeper I felt myself falling. A hole was growing around me, and I was on the verge of falling into it head first.

"Tell me," he growled. His hands moved so fast I hardly realized it until I felt them gripping me by the arms. His fingernails bit into my flesh... and as I looked at him... the color of his eyes, the small scar on the top of his head, the curve of his lips, and the darkness that shadowed his face... it made me realize reminding him of the past wouldn't do any good. Even if he remembered, it wouldn't make him the person I used to know. The person I had once loved. PGI Corp had taken that from me—from him.

My mind reeled for an answer, an excuse... anything. I could feel his grip growing tighter and tighter. The blood flow to my arms was gone as numbness took over my limbs. I needed to say something. The feral look in his eyes said if I didn't, I would very well be dead.

"I—" My voice stopped. What was I to tell him? I couldn't possibly tell him who I was. It was too early.

"Don't even think of lying to me because if you do, I will know. Then, when I find out that you did, I won't think to ask you what it was you lied about. I'll just make you bleed and make you hurt in the worst imaginable ways until your heart is no longer beating." There was nothing in the words he said to tell me he wasn't being honest.

I could feel my heart rate pick up, my mind scrambling for an answer. "You don't know me. You assume you do. It's obvious you're confused between your current memories and your past. I never met you before in my life."

I lied through my teeth, trying to show honesty in my eyes. If I shook even the slightest bit, if my eyes drifted away from his for a second, he would know it was a lie. In fact, I could bet anything that he expected me to lie.

"If you're lying to me..." He grit his teeth together, and I could hear the grinding of his molars. "I will fucking end you. Do you understand?"

I nodded my head, unable to say another word. I was too afraid I would confess the truth and my life would end in that instance. Looking at Killer, I desperately wanted to see Diesel. I wanted him to appear before me like the person he was before all of this.

He released me, and I watched his arms fall to his sides. His face was full of emotions that I was sure he didn't understand. He looked conflicted as if he wanted to hurt me, but something was telling him not to.

"I remember you though, you're in my mind..." his voice was a whisper.

"I'm not in your mind, you're just confused. Come on. We can talk about this on the way. Gauge gave us clearance to leave the building, but only together."

He grunted in anger. "When is he going to realize that whatever it is he is doing isn't fucking working? Talking to you annoys me and makes me angrier." He was irritated as usual, this scenario being a good example of said anger.

"It's not like I love being shackled up with you either," I murmured to him as we shuffled out of the room.

The tension between us was back to normal. It was then I wondered if I would ever be able to love him again.

Even more so, if the man I had fallen in love with to begin with was still in there.

Killer was just that... A killer. And Diesel was gone.

I had to come to grips with that.

thirteen

KILLER

I COULDN'T KEEP my eyes from watching the sway of her ass or the curve of her hips.

God, I needed to fuck someone, and I needed to fuck them hard.

I ran a hand through my hair. I knew Maggie was lying to me. She had to be. I didn't know what about or what it was she knew that she was clearly okay with dying over, but I wanted to know—and that alone kept her breathing.

"We can go get something to eat and then talk about these memories of yours." Her voice was soft, like the small cat they had given me in the holding cells at the treatment center. They wanted to see if we could handle something living without killing it. I strangled it. I remember its soft struggles against my hands as I squeezed the life out of it.

I grunted in response to her comment as she forced us through a crowd of people. The walls surrounding me were starting to break. I hated crowds, and I hated people just as much if not more.

"About these memories, what happens in them?" she asked as she curiously eyed me. We had spoken about the memories a time or two. Most of our time spent together was arguing or just not speaking. We tended to watch one another as we tried to gauge one another's expressions more than talking, though.

"You know what they're about..." She played dumb when she wanted to. That's what a lot of females would do. I realized it once we were released out into the regular population. She guided us to a hot dog stand that was on the curb. I found it strange to eat and order food in such a public environment. Maggie ordered for both of us knowing I wouldn't talk if she made me order my own.

With our food in hand we headed to a bench. It was nice to be free of the walls, but at the same time those walls were what protected me from losing it. They not only protected me from the people that hurt us, but they protected those outside of it. I was dangerous. It didn't matter what way you looked at it.

I ate the food Maggie gave me in less than two bites, all while she nibbled on hers nervously. Her eyes glided across the park. Would she try and make a run for it? Gauge had told me to keep an eye on her, that she might try to escape us. If she was thinking that she could out run me, or even out power me she had another think coming. I wasn't against hurting her in public again, even if I should've been. When it came to stopping someone from doing something I would do whatever I could.

"What are you thinking about?" I asked without evening thinking. Not once had I ever cared to ask her about her feelings or what it was that she was going through. Truthfully I didn't care, but more than that I didn't like the small talk associated with it. I learned that caring for others while in the cages did no good for me.

Her eyes shot up as if she had been caught thinking something she shouldn't. I could feel the smile forming on my face. I had caught her thinking of something that she knew would get her in trouble.

"Nothing, just that it's nice to be able to finally breathe air, to see the sun, and to feel the wind. Being held at that facility made me feel like I would never see another ounce of sunlight." Her voice faded out... as memories of my time in the cages surfaced.

"Inject him with more. I want to see blood seep from his hands. I want to create a monster that is so unstable no one will ever be able to reach him." The lab assistant said. I hated her. No, it was more than hate. I wanted her dead. I wanted her to suffer. To break her bones.

I watched as they entered the cage. I tried to step forward, but the darts they had used on me earlier caused me to grow weak. I strained against the chains that linked me to the wall. I wanted to laugh and scream all at the same time. If only I could get my hands on them, I would rip them to pieces.

"Killer..." The assistant smiled, and it was sickening. Even being the person I was right now, I knew how wrong it was for them to be doing this. To be taking those who were on their deathbeds and morphing them into something they never wanted to be.

Once you reach a certain level in your training, they give you a name. That name erases the number and to others, signifies your brutality. Only the best of us are named, the rest... well, the rest are stuck with their numbers as names.

"I now understand why they call you that. Dark hair, dark eyes. I would think you were good looking if you weren't a fucking monster." Her voice purred in satisfaction.

I flexed my fingers praying she would step just a little bit closer to me. Just close enough that I could wrap my hand around her throat and snuff out her pathetic life. Monster. She had no fucking clue what I was capable of doing.

I growled as I watched them load the gun full of one of their drugs of choice, the shit that would have me flying off the rails... I was sure, and as much as I hated it, I loved being able to let go. If only these chains would come undone.

"This won't hurt but a bit, Killer. Then you'll be back to your destructive ways." She smiled, but it

didn't meet her eyes. She aimed the gun at me and pulled the trigger.

I stared at her smiling as the dart landed on my exposed thigh. They would have another thing coming if I ever got out. Oh, how I would kill them, all of them. Their blood would spray against these walls. Their bones breaking would echo throughout this facility. Everyone would know the brutality they had caused once I was done.

Something was wrong. I blinked my eyes open and looked to the spot next to me.

Maggie.

She was gone, no sign of her. Fuck. I clenched my fists surveying the area. She must've waited for a memory to hit me. It made sense now, why she had asked me questions about the past. She wanted a way out.

I sniffed the air like a rabid dog as butterflies filled my stomach. Blood pumped to my cock at the thought of chasing her. I could take her. She had disobeyed me and disobeyed the very people who had saved my life. She was a liability, and now she would suffer whatever I felt was fit. I jumped from the bench, adrenaline from the memory and the hunt filling me.

I scanned the park looking for the nearest alley. If she were smart, she would try to stay low. I didn't know the city nearly as well as she did, but I had an advantage. I was made to kill, to hunt, and prey on those who failed to follow the rules. Right now, she was that prey. My eyes landed on the alleyway far off to the right. The park was situated between two buildings, and I knew she would've gone one of two ways.

I walked to the alleyway, and once I was out of sight, I started to run. My senses were heightened and were on the lookout for anything that could and would catch my attention. My breaths were precise, my fists locked and loaded. I could feel the need to kill creeping to the surface.

I hurried down another corridor and into another alleyway. I waited one second, then two... I could hear harsh breathing up ahead.

I smiled. A sick desire to mutilate and allow the monster just under the surface to break free. My steps were nimble as I moved. The breaths grew harsher and harsher. I could taste her fear in the air. Why had she run if she didn't want to be hurt?

"Maggie..." I taunted her. I wasn't sure why. It was the sick, fucked up part of me that wanted to drive her fear up and it did. I could feel the spike of energy in the air. Her breaths coming in and out, more like pants. Her hands were probably sweaty, and her eyes would be large brown orbs if I could see her right now.

Silence.

"If you didn't want me to hurt you, why did you run?" I cracked my knuckles, creeping over to the dumpster where I knew she was hiding. I circled around it before jumping forward and straight into her space. A startled scream threatened to leave her throat, but I ended it by placing a hand over her mouth. I cocked my head, examining her. She was beautiful, but she had to pay. She had broken the rules.

I gripped her tight around the waist pulling her body into my own as she bit at my hand. I pulled away out of reflex with an evil smile spread across my face.

"Let go of me," she growled, her fear now replaced with rage that mirrored my own. Her chest jutted out, and her body seemed to melt into mine. Didn't she know that I craved sex and pain? Blood and destruction?

My dick rose to attention at the very thought of fucking her senseless against this brick wall. Something inside of me said it was wrong, but with my hands on her hips, and her mouth moving, I couldn't think of anything better to do.

My grip on her grew harder. I could see her fighting against me. I could feel her trying to break free, and it just caused me to become harder. I would take, and continue to take until there was nothing left to take.

I shook my head as I gazed up into her eyes. Tears fell from them, her usual shade of brown growing darker. Pain marred her face as she continued to struggle against me.

"You're hurting me, Diesel," she screamed.

I bent down to her face, the scent of fear, sweat, and something else lingered in the air. That name! She said it again.

"Who is he?" I growled, shaking her. Her head bounced off the wall and a louder scream left her throat. I didn't care about anything other than the answers I needed.

"Please stop, please…" She whimpered. She was growing weak. Good, then I could get the answers I sought from her without having to worry about her trying anything that would make me want to kill her.

"WHO IS HE?"

My chest heaved against hers as I pushed her against the wall. She shook her head as the fear came off her in waves. I was done playing nice. I was done trying to ask.

I gripped her chin hard, forcing her to stare into my eyes. "If you don't tell me who he is, I will kill you. I won't threaten you anymore. I will wrap my hands around your beautiful neck and take in the scent of you as I trail my nose up and down it. Once I have your smell embedded into every aspect of who I am, I will suffocate you until you wish for death to take you. I will take from you what you're taking from me." I didn't even recognize my own voice.

"He…." The word left her lips, but I failed to hear the rest because a wave of nausea hit me, and then a memory so strong there was no letting go of it.

"They keep hurting me, Diesel." Her voice. I knew that voice. I looked down at the woman I was holding against the wall. Maggie.

"Let go, you're hurting me," she said again. I looked down at her arms, gazing at the red marks from where my fingers had dug into her delicate skin.

"I know…." The words fell from my lips but

seemed to stop there.

What was going on?

I felt the prick of a needle in my back and the surge of drugs entering my blood stream. My body began to grow heavy, my eyelids closing on their own.

"Killer..." Her cry hit my ears just as the darkness took me.

fourteen

MAGGIE

"LISTEN. DO YOU know how to do that, Maggie? Open your ears, and listen to what it is that I have to say." His words were forced, and I could see the straining of his muscles through the back of his shirt... I wiped the tears from my eyes. He was mad as hell as he had every right to be. He had saved my ass yet again, all because I was stupid enough to think that I could do this alone.

Tension formed between us as we walked further from the school and closer to the edge of the parking lot. He whirled around on me, and I almost fell over losing my balance.

"Why don't you see that your actions have consequences?" He reached out gripping my arm. His touch was harmless compared to the look he was giving me.

"I do see they have consequences, why don't you see that someday I will have to do it all alone anyway?" I threw my words at him hoping they hurt.

He was fuming angry, as was I. I could practically see the steam blowing out of his ears.

"That someday isn't right fucking now. Can't you—" he released me, walking away to the front of the car, where he landed a hard punch against the frame. I took a breath of air, filling my lungs. Violence wasn't the answer and wouldn't solve anything, just like acting out couldn't change the future. God had granted us limited time with one another, and I didn't want to spend the next hour arguing about who was right and who was wrong.

"Its fine, Diesel, you're right..." I trailed off.

"Get in the car," Diesel said gruffly, his back still to me.

"What? I drove here, I can take myself home," I told him, letting him know I didn't need his pity ride. He had saved me from Roger, but that didn't mean he owned me at every single turn.

"Get in the fucking car right now, or I will put you in the fucking car," he seethed. I took a step back and then rethought my actions.

He will just come and get you, I told myself.

Tucking my tail between my legs, I walked over to the passenger side door not even lifting my gaze to his. He unlocked it with the click of his key fob, and I slid into the seat.

Minutes passed as I watched him try to calm himself down. His face was a mass of emotions starting at anger and ending at confliction. When he got into the car, I could feel a change in him. It was as if he was done trying, done hiding from everything.

He shoved the key into the ignition bringing the engine to life. Diesel was like a broken piece of glass. Beautiful when the light reflected off it, but very capable of causing significant pain. All it would take was something small for him to cut you deep enough to bleed. You would feel the pain for a lifetime, the wound seeping blood with every pump of your heart.

"I'm sorry, I didn't mea—"

"Shut up, Maggie." He sounded as if he was just about to fall off that crazy train. I shivered in my seat forcing my attention out the window. I could feel the tears wanting to escape my eyes, but I forced them away. I wouldn't let him see the sadness that threatened to come undone every single day.

Ten minutes of silence had passed before I forced the words out of my mouth.

"You're an asshole, just so you know."

"As if I didn't know that already." His laugh filled the air.

"No, I honestly mean it. You're an asshole for expecting me to wait until you were long gone to move on with my life." The words left my mouth without a thought. He jerked the wheel forcing the car onto a gravel road. Once we were far enough from the road where no one could see us, he pulled over and threw the car into park.

He turned his body toward mine; hurt and betrayal could be found in his eyes. I wanted to reach out and to tell him I was sorry... but was I really?

"I'm an asshole for protecting you? Are you fucking kidding me?" I was confident he wanted to wring my neck. Or at least he looked like he wanted to anyway. Hell, I kind of wanted to wring my own neck for thinking that any of this could work.

"I didn't say you were an asshole for protecting me, but when does it end? When you're dead? When I'm forced to do it on my own? In case you forgot, you're dying. You're going to leave me here all alone..." I stifled the tears that wanted to pour from my eyes like rain. "When you die..." I took a deep breath, my chest aching, "I will be forced to move on with my life. I will be forced to do this alone, and I don't want to wait until then." I could feel the mask slipping from my face. The space inside the car was growing smaller and smaller like a box collapsing in on itself.

"Jesus, Maggie." Diesel's voice filled the space, commanding my attention. I turned to him, looking at him through my tears. My heart was breaking, my mind was a mess, and yet there was no one else I would rather have lost my shit in front of than him.

"Do you not think those very thoughts don't cross my mind every minute of every day? That one day I'll be dead, and all you will have left of me is a memory?" He slammed his fist down on the

dash. "Do you think I like knowing we love one another, but showing that emotion isn't worth it?" The words were pouring from his mouth, and for the first time in forever, I was startled into shock.

He turned, his eyes bleeding into my own. In them, I saw compassion, love, and fear. "If you think for one second it's the cancer that is going to kill me, you're wrong." I turned in my seat, not wanting to hear it anymore. I knew what he was going to say. I could feel it in my bones—in my soul.

"Look at me, damn it," he yelled. I couldn't contain the pain anymore. I opened the car door, leaving the car to get some air. The second I slammed the door behind me, I started walking away from the car. Not even a second later, I heard his door open. Did I really want to hear him say it? Could I even stand to hear the words?

"Run. Do it. Because that's what I have been trying to do this whole fucking time." He growled, taking huge steps toward me. His hand reached out gripping my arm and freezing me into place. He was my weakness, the very thing that made me tick. How cruel of a god it was to take the one thing that caused my heart to beat?

"If you think this cancer is killing me, you're wrong..." Water droplets fell from the sky landing on us and it was as if the heavens were finally crying as if they could feel our pain. His breath was warm against my face as he caressed my cheeks with the palms of his hands.

"It isn't the cancer that's killing me. It's loving

you. It's how I know that no matter how much I try to fight it, it will never go away. Knowing someday I won't be here anymore for you and knowing I love you with every fucking fiber of who I am and will never be able to move forward with you. I will never get to be a husband, a father..." I pushed him away, my heart breaking with every word he said.

"Stop!!" I screamed. I didn't want to hear it anymore. I shoved him away, but he held onto me, not letting me go.

"No, you stop. Stop fighting this, us. I have for so long... I have pushed it and you away for so long and there's no more denying it." I licked my lips and tipped my head back looking up at the sky. The rain continued to fall, covering our bodies. As much as I wanted to run, to hide, to let the pain evaporate into nothing, I couldn't. Something was holding me in place.

Diesel.

"I love you," he whispered. I couldn't even get a response in before his lips clashed with my own. In that kiss was everything he had never said to me before. His lips were harsh against mine as he placed one hand on my hip and used the other to tip my chin up. I could feel nothing but his love, his feelings, and him. He was everywhere.

His hands were all over me as he lifted me up, my legs wrapping around him instantly. Diesel walked us back toward the car, our lips never leaving one another's. My ass landed on the warm hood as I fought to suppress a moan. The heat against my cold skin was heaven.

"I want you. I have wanted you since you tried to stop Roger from bullying me on the bus." He shoved a piece of my hair behind my ear as he pressed his forehead against my own. I wanted him, too. Never had I wanted anything more, and even though I wanted to give in, I wasn't sure it was the right thing.

"I want you, too..."

"I can see it in your eyes. You're over thinking this. Yes, I'm dying, but you have known it this entire time. You had known it before your feelings changed into more, yet you didn't care."

I heard every word he spoke as if they were my own. He was right. I didn't care about him dying. If anything, it only made my love for him run deeper.

We had this very second, and I realized right then it wasn't worth it to fight it. It wasn't worth it to let the time go to waste. We had today. We could worry about tomorrow when it came.

He must've seen something in my eyes. It was in the next instance, my dress was being pushed up. Passion filled me as I watched him shove my panties down. He wanted me just as much as I wanted him.

"I'll try to be gentle." He laid a soft kiss on my shoulder as he pushed the top of my dress down, revealing my breasts. I smiled, staring up at the sky. The rain was cold against my skin, but it told me something—it told me I was alive.

"Don't try to be gentle, don't be anything less

than what you are. I want you, Diesel. I want every single part of you." My voice was so soft, I wasn't sure it was my own. He smiled, placing a hard kiss against my lips. With a flick of his fingers, he unbuttoned his pants and pushed down his underwear.

"Maggie..." He sighed as he said my name and slipped his hand between my legs. I could feel his fingers trailing up my inner thigh as he slipped one into my hot core. I tensed as the invasion was foreign. *"I will always remember this moment with you. I will never forget you, or what you gave me."* He stroked me softly and slowly, allowing me to grow accustomed to his finger before adding another. With every shove and push of his fingers, I could feel myself growing hot all over, the warmth deep in my belly spreading.

"It feels so good," I cried out, letting him know whatever he was doing was working. I had never felt so free in my entire life.

"You feel so good, come for me. Let go so I can watch you come for me," he whispered. His words were my undoing. My toes curled, stars flashed before my eyes, and it was as if I were feeling everything for the first time. His hands, his mouth, the warmth of his skin, the rain droplets... everything.

His fingers pulled out of me, and I opened my eyes, peering up at him as he reached into his back pocket. *"Did you think you were going to get lucky?"* I joked, watching him pull a condom from his wallet. He flashed me a soft smile as he ripped the package open with his teeth.

"I'm dying, I'm not dead." I would've laughed at his comment had my eyes not locked on his cock. It was large, larger than anything I had ever seen. I clamped up right then and there, unsure of how this was going to work. His fingers hadn't hurt, but his fingers didn't look like that.

"Shhh... it's going to be okay. I'll enter you slowly. You tell me if it hurts, okay?" He tried to soothe my nervousness with calming words, but the more I stared at his cock, the more tense I grew.

He rolled the condom on and then pulled my ass to the edge of the hood as he centered himself at my entrance. This wasn't how I had ever pictured losing my virginity, but it was with Diesel, and to me, that was more than perfect.

"Ready?" he asked, hunger glittering in his eyes. I nodded my head yes, smiling. The smile fell the second he pushed the head in. There was a sting of pain, the feeling of being ripped in half.

"I can't..." I cried out, taking a deep breath. He stopped me from turning away from him by cupping the side of my face and pulling it more into his.

"You can, I got you." His voice was sincere. Sweat coated his brow, and I knew he was holding back. He was straining not to slam into me.

"Okay..." I mumbled against his cheek allowing him to push in more. In one swift movement, he was in. Burning spread through my core and the overwhelming pressure of fullness.

My chest constricted, a heaviness filling it.

Deep breaths. I told myself this as he stroked my hair.

"Are you okay?" he asked. I nodded my head yes again as tears sprung from my eyes and mixed with the rain. He waited a few minutes before pulling out and pushing back in. Pain spread through my core, but I gritted my teeth telling myself the pain was a good thing. It was a memory of Diesel I wouldn't just remember, but I would have felt it.

"So fucking good..." he growled, peppering kisses across my chest. My body ached, and I knew I wasn't going to get anything from this.

"Please tell me you're almost there..." I cried out in pain.

"Almost baby, almost..." he cried out, holding my body tight to his. I could feel his heartbeat rise, his cock growing and pulsing inside of me. The feeling was exhilarating, and that alone pushed the discomfort to the back of my mind. Never in my life had I thought I would have a moment as beautiful as this one.

"I love you..." The words fell from my lips like a whisper.

Raindrops fell from Diesel's hair as he stared down at me. "You're my reason for breathing, my life."

fifteen

KILLER

FUCK. THAT ONE single word bounced off the walls inside of my head. An overbearing sense of heaviness flowed through my arms and legs as the echoes from that word caused me to stir awake. My mouth was as dry as cotton, and as I tried to swirl my tongue around to produce saliva, I could hear the rattling of chains and the smell... what was that smell?

Somehow, I knew that smell. Clean, sterilized, with a lingering hint of alcohol. Like a doctor's office but ten times worse.

Memories floated back into my mind. I was chasing after Maggie. I had cornered her... *Maggie*. My chest constricted as I tried to sit up. I forced my eyelids open not wanting to look, but knowing where I was before I even saw the dim glow of the overhead lights.

"Welcome back, Killer." I shifted, my body going ramrod straight. Blood pumped into my ears as a fire stirred in my belly. We were here, and Maggie was missing. My eyes searched my surroundings, looking for any evidence of a struggle.

"If you're looking for the girl, she's here... just not in your cell," the lab assistant wearing a white coat said. Bars surrounded me, in front and back, cement walls replaced the bars to my left and right, and a door off to the right looked as if it were sealed, all to keep me captive. I narrowed my eyes, focusing on the lettering embroidered into the fabric. *PGI Corp.* Somewhere in my mind, a small spark was ignited. Those three letters and one word sounded vaguely familiar.

"Just... give her to me." I didn't want to beg. To let them know she meant something to me when, in reality, she could never mean anything to me. I just knew this place well enough to know someone as fragile as her wouldn't survive without me. I was a monster, but I wasn't that horrible to make her into something she never asked to be. Never would she be subjected to the testing I had been if I had a say in it.

"Give her to you? Come on, Killer. We both know you realize how this works. You follow the orders and you get what you want. You disobey, and, well..." The dickhead's voice grew dark, and the doors behind him opened revealing a very knocked out Maggie in the arms of another man.

I gritted my teeth, forcing myself not to lash out. I didn't want to know what they needed from me. What they wanted me to do...

"We will give her to you, under one condition," the dickhead said. I was unable to take my eyes off her, watching her chest rise and fall. If she died, there would be no saving me. I would go off the rails. She might not have been anything important, but she was now my only way of staying human. I would hold onto her humanity, living through it to keep me sane in this place. It was my only hope.

"Don't fuck with me, douche bag. Get to the point." I cracked my knuckles, showing him I was up for anything. My muscles ached, and my legs still felt like they were tied to cement blocks at the bottom of the ocean.

Dickhead smiled, and I desperately wished he were close enough for me to reach through the bars and grip him by the throat. Would he scream in fear?

"When we have everything from her... we need you to do us a favor... Better yet, when the time comes, we need you to do something." The smirk was still on his face. I growled. I didn't like not knowing what I had to agree to.

"What do you want?" I barely got out, my eyes still trained on Maggie's lifeless body. "We want you to kill her." My eyes grew wide, and my chest cracked. I could feel something breaking inside of me. I had thought many times about killing her, about ripping her throat out, suffocating her. Yet, I had never been able to cross the line. I had never been able to make it more than a thought. The memories always stopped me. Looking at her now, I knew I wouldn't be able to do it and that alone would be the very thing that got us both killed.

"Why?" I tried to sound curious, and less worried about what they would do to the two of us if I couldn't follow through. The truth was it didn't matter if I killed her or not because they wouldn't let me go. Dickhead looked at me sideways before wrapping a finger around one of Maggie's dark brown locks of hair.

"See, she knows some stuff. Stuff that could hurt this corporation, even you, so we want to put a stop to it. Kill her... and earn your freedom, fail to do so and face the consequences..."

I looked around the room, my eyes scanning for a way out. There had to be a way to escape. The cell I was in was new—hell, the facility in itself was new. Besides the bars keeping me prisoner, a pair of sliding glass doors that lead into a chamber separated us. That chamber must have been where they had kept Maggie. I could feel the tension filtering into my mind, the anger, rage, and hate coming back to me tenfold.

They wanted me to kill her, could I do it...?

"I'll do it." I agreed knowing there was no way for me to do it. Somehow, someway, I would have to find another way out. Either that or the Brotherhood would have to find us. The sealed door to my cell opened as Dickhead pressed his hand to a small screen next to the door. That was also new. I watched as he pulled a key from his pocket and placed it into the lock hole.

"Stay against the wall. If you take one step, we shoot her up with more L1 than her fragile body can handle," Dickhead raged. The door slid upward with a loud creak. For one second, I considered charging them, using my body weight to my advantage. Then again, it would be useless. This was a new facility I was unfamiliar with, and they had more power than I had. I was strong alone in myself, but when it came to twenty-to-one, they would always win, plus they would shoot us both up. Instead, I pressed my heels to the back of the wall as the man holding her squatted down just enough to place Maggie against the concrete and roll her into my cell.

The moment her body landed on the floor safely, I charged forward causing the man to jerk upward, smacking his head against the bottom of the steel sliding door. I growled in acceptance of his pain knowing deep down every person in this building feared me. The man backed away as I watched the door slide back down locking me inside with Maggie. "Try something like that again, and you won't have to worry about killing her—we'll do it for you," Dickhead said. He moved away from the panel that I now knew controlled the door to the cell. Funny how he could say those things to me while bars separated us. If he had no escape and no protection from me, he would be pissing his pants by now and begging me to spare him.

My thoughts spiraled out of control as I inched my way over to where Maggie was. Her body was

P a g e | 161

lying on the cold floor, and as I touched her hand, I could feel the coldness of the room seeping into her skin.

This place will steal her warmth, her goodness.

I gripped both her arms and dragged her carefully over to the corner. Staring at her, I tried to figure out what to do. They hadn't given us blankets or pillows. They never provided us with anything other than the things that were needed to keep us alive. My eyes glided over her body and then to the confines of our new home.

Fuck. I wanted to scream. What was I supposed to do? It wasn't in my nature to care and protect, but here I was trying to find a way to keep her alive...

You have to... a small voice inside my head whispered. Gritting my teeth, I pushed to the wall and slid down. Maggie's head was right next to my thigh. With little effort, I could cradle her body in my arms allowing my warmth to protect her. I shuddered at the mere thought.

This isn't the real me. I can't do this... Blood spilled from my fingertips as I tried to dig them into the concrete floor. I didn't want to do this.

What if I hurt her? I asked myself the question even though I already knew the answer. I wouldn't. Not just that, but I couldn't. She was our ticket out of here alive. Pushing all doubt to the back of my mind, I gripped her as gently as I could and pulled her into my chest. She stirred slightly, her face rubbing into my chest muscles. Warmth bloomed somewhere deep inside of me, melting a sliver of

P a g e | **162**

the coldness that had made me who I was. Clutching her as if she was going to disappear, I closed my own eyes and allowed myself to revel in the feelings of her small body in my arms. Her breath mixed with my own caused our scents to mingle together. Every breath I took calmed the demon inside of me.

Minutes passed in silence as my breath evened out. I wasn't sure what was going to happen to the two of us. I had been here, in this place, once before. Maggie hadn't. She had no sense or idea of what this place was about.

I could feel the memories poking at my shields wanting badly to knock them down, but I couldn't let them. I couldn't let my guard down for one second. Doing so was what had gotten us here to begin with.

Fuck. I opened my eyes and looked down at Maggie. She was beautiful, something I had known this entire time. She was also familiar, in a sense that my body and mind called to her. Somehow, she knew me. I could feel it deep inside of me because whenever she was around, the person within always tried to escape.

Allowing my eyes to drift back closed, I saw Maggie in my mind. Memories swirled around me until I could no longer shake them. I was being pushed into a dark tunnel with no light at the end.

"I loved you, Diesel. I loved you more than life itself." I could hear the emotion in her words and all but see the tears running down her face. *What was happening? Maggie! I screamed out, but it*

was all inside my head. I couldn't move, yet I was awake. More and more people gave their graces, and it was then that I realized I was at a funeral.

Not just anyone's but my own.

I tried to fight against the numbness that was radiating throughout my body. My lips wouldn't move, and my eyes refused to open. Panic seized me. Was my chest moving with every intake of breath I took? How could I be here but not be here?

"Diesel was a great kid, a great person..." I could hear my dad's voice. He was speaking at my funeral. Squeezing my eyes tighter, trying to push past this... My mind went blank. I could feel time moving and when I finally popped my eyes open, I was lying in a hospital bed. My parents were talking about me.

"He's out of control, Jane. He won't let the nurses care for him, and I know he said he wanted to get better, but it's too late. The cancer has spread to other parts of his body." My eyes scanned the room. My mom clasped her hands together, her eyes roaming over me.

"I just don't want to give up on him. I don't want him to die if there is a chance he could come out of this on the other end. He's our only child." My mother's face was red and streaked with tears. I wanted to reach out to her and comfort her. I had never truly hated my parents. I was just annoyed that they felt they could force their beliefs on me. They just didn't want to lose me, just as I didn't want to lose Maggie.

MAGGIE!!! I screamed out, thrashing about

the bed. I needed to get to her, to explain what was happening.

"Then it's settled, we give him to the corporation. They can use him and better understand his behavior. He's already a lost cause."

No, I'm not! I screamed the words, yet they couldn't be heard. What was happening? Pain slammed into my head as I was transported to another memory.

"I just wanted to be able to say goodbye. I just wanted to be able to hold you one last time. To tell you that the love you had given me will make me search for a cure in your name. For the rest of my life, you will live on in my heart. You're mine." Tears formed in my eyes but never spilled over.

There was no wetness seeping from my eyes, no heart beating in my chest, or breath leaving my lips.

No!!!! What was happening? I couldn't lose her. I did all this for her. I sought out going to the hospital for treatments for her. She had given me a reason to live. For the first time in my life, I wanted to see tomorrow.

My chest heaved as something inside my head clicked. My eyes fluttered closed, and then opened again. I could feel warmth from the inside, warming me all over. Starting in my arms and coursing through my entire body. I felt something deeper than rage and anger. I felt... it was a foreign emotion, one I hadn't felt in years—love?

I looked down at the woman in my arms.

Maggie.

A sigh escaped my lips. She had found me. She had to have known all along. But, why wouldn't she tell me? At this moment in time, her reasons for keeping quiet no longer mattered because now I remembered. I remembered everything that was Diesel and Mags.

Everything that was she and I.

I knew who I was, what I once was to her, and what I needed to do to get us the fuck out of here.

sixteen

MAGGIE

WHEN I AWOKE, my mouth was dry, and my neck felt as if it had been snapped. Deep warmth engulfed me, and I almost didn't want to move. I could feel a heartbeat under my hands and deep breaths blowing against my face.

Killer. The memories of what had happened came back to me, and immediately, I regretted having run from him. I desperately wanted Killer to remember me, but I was tired of feeling trapped. I was scared and alone, and I just wanted a way out. Therefore, when I was given the chance, I ran... I didn't realize how dangerous that one decision was.

When I forced my eyes to open, I was met with a shade of blue eyes I hadn't seen in years. Somehow, some way, I knew those eyes belonged to the man who I had loved all those years ago and still loved today.

"Diesel?" I said his name in questioning slightly afraid it would trigger something inside him if I were wrong. With one look, I knew it was Diesel. I couldn't believe he was here and Killer was gone. My heart rate skyrocketed as he smiled at me.

"Mags." My name coming from his lips caused me to grip him. I had to feel him to make sure he was truly here. He still looked like Killer, but he wasn't. His smile was genuine, his voice calm and soft. This was him. It wasn't a lie or my mind playing jokes on me. He was truly here. He had found his way back to me through the rage, hate, anger, and the need to kill.

"This is really you? You're here? Are you going to disappear?" I asked eagerly, my words coming out in a rapid rush. I didn't know how to handle the emotions that were running through me. Instead, I sat up in his lap and wrapped my arms around him.

"This is really me. I'm here and I remember everything." Guilt could be heard heavily in his words as he ran his hand down my hair. I never stopped to think about what would happen if Diesel came back if he remembered everything. If he would be able to handle the guilt of all he had done. Most of which I had no idea of.

"God... Thank you God," I cried out, burying my face in his neck. He smelt of sweat, man, and home. He smelt like everything I ever wanted and needed.

"I missed you so fucking much. I'm sorry, so fucking sorry for hurting you. For talking down to you," he whispered into my ear and then nuzzled into my neck. It was as if I had never lost him. As if time had never separated us from one another.

"Shhh... It's okay. You're here now. I did all this for you. We found each other again. Everything is going to be okay now," I mumbled. We had things that we needed to talk about. I needed to tell him things that he should know. I wanted answers to what happened to him, but somewhere deep inside of me, I knew everything would be okay because we had each other again.

"I remember it all. The funeral, the hospital. I remember my parents faking my death and giving me to this fucking place to be turned into a guinea pig. I remember everything." His voice broke, and so did something else in me. Nothing else mattered in this second. I knew that death could very well happen. I knew if someone wanted to, they could hurt us both.

Where we were wasn't important right now though. It was who we were.

"It's okay, it's okay. We have to stay strong." I soothed him. Seeing the faraway look in his eyes scared me. I was afraid I would lose him at any second.

"It will be." His chest heaved against mine as he eased off me and came to a standing position. Even the way he looked and carried himself was different. His eyes scanned our surroundings, and I wanted to ask him what he was looking for, but he answered me before I could cough out the words.

"Cameras. They have them here. I know they do." He growled. With jerky movements, I made it to my feet and wiped my sweaty palms on my jeans.

"Stop trying to find them. It's not going to do us any good. We need to focus on getting out of here." I approached him calmly, keeping my voice neutral. I was two feet away from him when he whirled around on me. His eyes were still the same, and when he reached out and wrapped his hand into my hair, I knew he wasn't going to go anywhere.

"I'm so fucking sorry about all of this…" He was repeating himself. I knew the second he came back to life, he would be the man I had always known, but he would have blood on his hands and a lot of it.

"Don't be." I placed my lips against his, sealing whatever apology he was going to come up with away. I didn't want to hear about the bad things he had done. I wanted to live in the moment.

His lips ravished mine as he moved us to the nearest cement wall. Gone were his thoughts on the cameras, on the people who had placed us in here.

"I have prayed for years to feel your lips against my own again." It was almost as if he was saying a silent prayer with his lips. My hand found its way into his hair, the dark locks weaving through my fingers.

"I love you," he huffed out, his chest pressing against my own as he picked me up forcing me to wrap my legs around him. Unable to form words, I allowed him to kiss down my neck and over my chest. His body was doing funny things to my mind. I wanted him to take me, to fuck me in front of all these people. It didn't matter to me anymore. I had waited so long for this to happen.

"Take me..." I begged. I just wanted him. The man he was right here, in this second, to make love to me. My body longed for him more than anything in the world. He pulled away, a mischievous smile on his face.

"Give me time, Mags. I'm not ready to take you yet, that is unless you want me to unleash everything out on you." The thought excited me and frightened me at the same time. What if I lost him in the moment?

"I just missed you, I want you. I longed for your voice, your touch, your kisses, even your scent. You have no idea what it does to me to sit next to you and to know you're in there somewhere, yet the man that is on display before me is unlike yourself."

His hips ground into me, causing a delicious rush of pleasure to form inside of me. Words were lost as he nipped at my earlobe.

"Believe me, Maggie. I know what it's like. I know what it's like to watch from the inside and beat against the glass as hard as you can, begging yourself to remember. The fact I had to watch myself almost kill you..." His words cut off.

"It's going to be okay. I'm sorry I brought it up." I cursed myself for ruining the moment. Everything else in that second was completely fucked up. All I wanted was one joyous moment before it got worse.

"Never be sorry." He cupped the side of my cheek. Apprehension settled deep into my belly. Not only was I uncertain of what the future was going to hold for Diesel and me, but I was terrified we wouldn't even make it out of here alive.

"Step to the back of the cell." A voice startled me as it boomed into the cell vibrating off the walls and bars. Immediately, Diesel removed his hands from me and shoved us against the nearest wall, his back to my front. Fury grew around us. It was as if they merely being near us fueled the beast inside of him. His hand shot back gripping my arm to hold me into place.

"Stay back," he growled his voice animalistic. Trying as I may, I peeked through Killer's arm and body, my mouth dropping open. On the opposite side of the bars stood Roger with someone behind him.

"Awe. Is Killer back to his usual self?" Roger began to goad him. I was unable to speak or process what was really happening.

"Wait, maybe I should call you Diesel now since that is your name, right? Which, by the way, since you decided to surprise us with your appearance on this fine day, I have a surprise for you, too. Did you tell him already, Mags?" Roger saying my name, using the very nickname Diesel always called me, caused my stomach to quake in fear. What was he going to try to do?

"Don't. Don't even utter her name again... You're not worthy enough to even speak her name." Diesel was on the verge of losing his temper as Killer teetered on the edge of his sanity. I felt like I was about to lose both of them.

"Put the claws away, macho. I have someone else here for you. Come on, Richard," Roger said, gesturing for the man to move from behind him. My eyes locked on his face, and instantly, my blood turned cold.

"Dad?" I was so astonished that the air left my chest immediately as dread set in. What was my father doing here? Better yet, what was Roger doing ordering him around? He smiled softly as Roger turned around and gripped him by the arm, shoving him toward us. What a coward. Silence passed between all of us, and as my eyes came back to meet Roger's, it was then I understood what he was doing. He was using us. Killer, my dad, and me.

"I never meant for things to get this out of hand. I never wanted any of this," Dad cried out. He sounded like he was begging for forgiveness—but why? He hadn't done anything wrong.

"Dad, I don't—"

"What is going on, Maggie?" Diesel cut me off as I pulled away from him. His eyes zeroing in on me like prey, I could feel Killer's presence entering and Diesel's disappearing more and more.

"I don't know." I shook my head, confusion setting in.

"Isn't this sweet? A family reunion." Roger shoved my dad another step forward causing Killer to growl and my heart to drop into the pit of my stomach. Diesel was fading and fading fast. I could hear his teeth grinding together from the rage that was on the very surface of being unleashed.

"I don't understand." Diesel sounded conflicted as he fought internally against himself. I had no logical answer to what was going on. I was just as lost as he was.

"Oh, you mean she hasn't told you yet?" Roger's eyes promised hurt. My skin was crawling as he stared at me. I could feel Diesel pulling from me, my body growing cold at his absence.

"Wait I don't—"

"Don't lie, Maggie." Roger laughed, his voice filling the small room. It echoed off the walls, causing a splitting ache to form in my head. He was framing me... turning us against each other.

"What is he talking about?" He turned around, facing me. Diesel no longer visible. He was no longer the man I had known just moments ago. He was Killer in all his bloody fucking glory. I wanted to hold my hands up in defense, to protect myself from this beast of a man who stood before me, but it was no use. If he wanted to hurt me, he would.

"I don't even know." I could feel my lip quivering, terror growing inside of me.

"You don't know?" Killer crossed the distance between us gripping me by the throat and pressing me against the wall so fast, my neck snapped back and my head bounced off the cement. Stars formed in my eyes, and I could taste blood in my mouth.

"Oh, the joy. See, Maggie there has been hiding a secret from you. Her and her father work for me. This whole time it's been nothing but a ploy to get you back here. I mean, you were our most accomplished project of them all."

Tears formed in my eyes as the grip Killer had on my throat increased. I could feel the oxygen deprivation taking me. I clawed at his hands, my attempts fruitless.

"I don't believe you." Killer growled immediately after the words left his mouth. He was at war with himself. Fighting man against monster. Diesel against Killer as his eyes shifted between the two of us.

Roger laughed again, but this time it was darker, "I don't care if you believe me. In reality, you don't really care either since you're three seconds away from killing her anyway." I could feel the hold on my throat loosen, and I took that moment to breathe, gasping in a breath.

"Tell me it's a lie, Maggie. Tell me that this isn't true." Tears fell from my cheeks as he stared into my eyes. How could I tell him that I had done all of this for him? That the very reason I was here in the first place was to find a cure?

"I can explain, I'm not really—"

"TELL ME THE FUCKING TRUTH!" he screamed in my face. I couldn't form a word, nor could I swallow, my mind on autopilot, my eyes trained on him.

"I can smell your fear..." Killer leaned into me, his nose skimming up and down the sensitive skin of my neck. "I can taste it." His tongue darted out and licked a path from my earlobe to my collarbone. My breath hitched, my heart beat faster, and my pulse jumped out of my throat and into my stomach.

"Why is it so hard to believe? Little Maggie isn't the saint you made her out to be. I mean, I could've told you that. The way she sucked my cock..."

"ENOUGH!" Killer bellowed, his voice like thunder. His hand had tightened on my throat before he asked again.

"Tell me the truth, Maggie. Tell me that he's lying, and I'll take all the pain away." I could see Diesel beneath the surface fighting for us. He wanted to believe that I hadn't sided with the company who took his life from him. Who took me from him.

"I'm sorry, I'm so sorry, Killer. I didn't know. I swear, I had nowhere else to go, and I needed the money." I cried, not only for us, but for the loss of him as I watched his eyes shut, and his world go dark. Most of all, I cried because I truthfully did all of this for him.

Panic gripped me as the hand at my throat grew tighter and tighter. My father's screams echoed around me, and I could still see the sick smile on Roger's face. After all, he had gotten what he wanted... He wanted to break him. To pin us against one another.

"Release her—I want her," Roger said. My eyes grew wide as a smile formed on Killer's face. It was the scariest thing I had ever seen.

"Sure, take the bitch. She's no fucking better than the rest of you." He released me, stepping away as I slid down the wall. Air filled my lungs as tears escaped my eyes. My heart was breaking—shattering. There would be no starting over. There would be no finding peace with the man I loved because the man I loved was once again gone.

Roger glanced over at the lab assistant, and

with one nod, the steel door lifted and he swooped in, pulling me up onto my unsteady legs and onto the other side of the bars by my hair. The pain in my scalp didn't register to me nearly as much as the pain in my heart. I would rather be beaten over and over again than to have him look at me as if I were the enemy.

"No problem… I'll take good care of her," Roger commented.

"Take her, but just know that she is mine to fucking kill. She is mine to end. And Maggie…" The way my name slid off his tongue caused me to take a step back, pushing further into Rogers's chest. "I will kill you. You can run, you can hide, you can cry, you can even beg me to spare your life, but just know that I will be the reason you take your last breath."

It was with those words and the lack of life in his eyes that made me realize, for the first time in my life, I was afraid of the man that I loved. I knew if he got his hands on me again, he would, in fact, end my life with a twist of his wrist.

"Perfect, you can kill her later. I have some things I want to get out of her first." Roger gripped my hair tighter, pulling me toward the sliding glass doors behind us.

"You know what to do, Richard," Roger added. I could see the sick smile creeping onto Killer's face as my father entered his cell.

"I'll be sure to kill Daddy dearest first…" A sob escaped my throat as I saw the terror fill my father's eyes. I didn't know if I would ever be able to forgive

Killer if he harmed my father. I would never be able to look at him the same.

"Please don't," I begged out of thin air as Killer's smile grew even more.

"I'll enjoy every fucking second of it. Then I'll come for you next." He lurched forward just as the door slid down, my father on the wrong side of the bars.

"Please don't do this, Roger, please don't." I huffed the words out, my heart beating out of my chest.

"Now, now, Maggie." He tried to soothe me with his words, but it wasn't enough. I didn't want him. Then I felt the prick in my arm and the world around me growing dark. I wanted to fight against it, but I didn't. Instead, I allowed myself to freefall into the darkness.

There was no hope for me. I had lost Diesel, and Killer was out for blood.

seventeen

KILLER

THE LIGHT BEHIND my eyes was dark. I forced oxygen in and out of my lungs. I couldn't escape the darkness that was threatening to take me. Her scream, the fear in her eyes showed me just how dark I needed to be just to save her. I was losing the grasp of who I truly was and transforming into a monster.

"Just calm down, Killer. Breathe, deep breaths," the small man before me said. He was wearing a lab coat. He was no better than the others were. My fists clenched, tension building in my muscles. I needed to unleash the beast. I needed blood on my hands. I wanted to laugh in this man's face. Who did he think he was?

"Calm down?" My chest rumbled with laughter. "Calm isn't my kind of thing, and since I discovered

PROJECT: k i l l e r

you and that bitch daughter of yours are working together, I really can't do calm. However, I can plan your funeral. Would you prefer open casket or closed? I'm thinking closed for your family's sake. "

I watched his eyes grow wide as he took a step back. I was seething with rage. How could she do this to us? To the very fragile ground that we stood upon?

"She didn't do anything wrong..." Of course, he would stick up for her. He was her father. He created the vindictive bitch.

"Her still breathing is wrong, her still living and having even known me is wrong. Was this a set up from the start?" I questioned, teetering right on the edge of sanity. I wanted to fuck her into oblivion and then watch her bleed out. I wouldn't make her death quick. No, I would draw it out, inflicting pain in ways that were unimaginable.

"Killer, listen to me. Please, listen. She did this for you. She worked at this place—she didn't work in the labs. She worked in the offices. She has no idea what this place is about." His words were fucking with my head. I could feel fuzziness going in and out like a TV with a bad connection.

"She didn't do this for me." I could barely get the words out. Something in my chest was cracking—breaking. My chest burned, my heart ached, and I could feel something deep within me struggling to break free.

"She did. I have a plan. A way out, but I need you to calm down. To be level headed." His voice was so quiet I almost didn't hear it.

P a g e | **180**

j.l. beck

It's a lie. A trap. The words echoed around in my mind.

"STOP LYING!!" I screamed, beating my fist against my head.

"There are cameras in every inch of this room. You fell right into Roger's trap without even thinking. You hurt the one person you loved more than life itself, and for what? Did you get satisfaction out of it?"

"STOP!" I screamed, my chest heaving with every breath.

"I won't stop. I know that you're in there. I know you'll regret this all when you come to the realization that we did nothing wrong."

"You're doing wrong as we speak. You engaging in conversation with me is wrong..." I was snapping, fracturing into someone else.

"I will make you all pay. I will bring this building and everyone in it to the fucking ground. Do you hear me?" I screamed, grabbing the bars of the cell.

"Your fighting is useless..." I turned on him, my anger directed at his mere presence.

"I will kill you, but not until I kill your daughter first. She betrayed me when I offered her my love. I will torture you both. I will teach you both that fucking with me was the wrong thing to do. You woke the beast, and now he's thirsty for blood." My voice cracked as I took another step toward him.

His blood would be on my hands.

"Killer." He didn't sound scared or worried. He just looked like he was annoyed.

"Richard, any last words?" I sneered.

"No, any last words, Killer?" he asked as I came to a stand in front of him, my hand reaching out to grip him by the throat.

I narrowed my eyes at him, and then realized I had been fooled. I could feel the prick of the needle against my skin. The drugs surging through my body. He had fooled me—they all had.

"I'm sorry. I wanted to do this any other way than the current, but you just wouldn't listen." He looked hurt as if doing this to me was the last thing he ever wanted to do.

Weakness took over as my fingers became numb, relaxing around his throat before falling to my sides. My eyes drifted closed as I tried to fight the drugs.

"When you wake up, we can talk, we can discuss this further..." Rage seethed within me. He was wrong—once I woke up, I would destroy and kill everything in my power.

Somewhere in my mind, I clung to a memory. A memory that caused me to rethink everything I had ever done.

"Why're you mad at me?" I wanted answers. To beg her to tell me what was wrong. I had gone so long hiding my emotions that I wasn't sure how to handle the feelings that I had now.

"I'm not mad," she huffed.

"Yes, you are," I countered back.

"Diesel." The way she said my name with warning had my cock growing hard. I prayed that in death, I would find peace. I also hoped God

would allow me to wait for Maggie at Heaven's gate.

"Mags." I said her name with just as much warning, raising my eyebrow up at her. This tug of war game we played was amusing, yet frustrating at the same time. She knew all the right buttons to push on me.

"I don't want you to feel guilty for giving into me. For giving us a chance. I don't want you to think that when you die, you're leaving me here all to my lonesome because you're not." What she was saying caused a stirring in my chest. My heart rate accelerated. I could never force myself to think about what would come.

"Look at me." She placed her small hand against my cheek. The warmth of her hand against my skin made me want to sink into her touch. The days were growing endless, and I knew that one day I wouldn't wake up. I needed to treat every touch of her skin as a remembrance allowing her to heal me from the outside in. She didn't know it, but she cleansed me.

"I regret nothing. I don't regret the fact that I have gotten to know you. That I learned what makes you tick. That I touched you and devoured you in ways that were unimaginable. I don't blame God for bringing you into my life. You made me whole, Maggie. You brought the best out in me, even when I didn't think it was there."

Her soft sigh reminded me of what it was like to live, to feel, to be alive.

"I just don't want you to feel guilty. I don't

want you to be on your deathbed and question if it was the right thing. I don't want to be seen in your eyes at the end of all of this as guilt."

I leaned into her, her smell surrounding me, calling to me in ways I never thought possible. My lips pressed softly against her forehead. Never would she be an object of guilt. No, she would just be mine.

"You will never be seen as guilt. You will always be seen as my Mags. The woman who opened my heart to new things, and allowed the man who was dying inside to live on the outside. You gave me one last chance at love."

"I love you, Diesel. I love you for loving me, for protecting me, and I'm going to miss you more than anything when you're gone." I could all but see the tears streaking her face. She would be lost without me. Hurting. Broken even. But somehow she would find the strength to carry on, and in her, she would carry my spirit—my love.

"When the time comes, you will know. You will never be alone, Maggie. You will never fear anything. I will be right beside you—inside you. Breathing the same air as you and matching the beat of your own heart. We are one being. One soul in two different realms. Do you understand that this isn't the end? It's simply goodbye... for now. Not forever. Not when I'm in here." I pointed to her heart.

She moved in my arms, her tears smearing against my shirt. I could hear her quiet sob and understood her pain.

j.l. beck

"I don't want to lose you after just having found you. I don't want this to end." She bawled into my shirt, her fists squeezed tightly as she brought them up to my chest. I could feel the tremors running through her body as she fought for control over her emotions, and a soft smile crested my lips.

She was living, she was feeling, and that's all I ever wanted for her.

"It will be okay. It'll be like a band-aid. It will hurt really badly in the beginning, like when you're first pulling it off, but then after a while the pain will subside. You'll look at where the band-aid was and remember the pain you felt, but will feel no longer and you'll remember the scar that the pain created."

"I don't want to lose you." She cried harder.

"You're not losing me."

"Yes, I am. You're leaving. I won't be able to touch you, feel you, or kiss you anymore. I won't get to laugh with you anymore, and I will be so alone. I'll lose my best friend—my everything." I held her against my chest.

"Someday, you'll look back on this and laugh. I promise," I mumbled into her ear, her hair blowing against my face.

"Nothing about losing you is funny. You're dying, Diesel. Dead, gone. Part of the ground." She was freaking out, which was normal, but I had finally found peace. Not just that—but I had a plan. I wanted to be able to be here, but there was no way I could tell her that. If the day came it all *worked out, then I would. I just needed to admit that I needed the treatments, and I needed to pray that it would give me just a little bit more time with her.*

"Whatever happens, you will always be mine."

"There is no whatever happens. Death will happen. It will take you from me without notice. That is what will happen." I rubbed my hand across her back and pulled her in tighter wanting us to become one. Then I placed another kiss against her skin and reveled in the feeling of love.

She was it. She was love.

eighteen

MAGGIE

"YOU'RE SUCH A slut, Maggie. How could you put out to Roger not even two days after your boyfriend's death." The insults were hurled at me left and right. Their lies penetrating my truths. The pain inside of me radiating outward. I just wanted it to stop.

"Wake up, you stupid bitch." I could feel a burning in my face as a hit landed against my cheek. I forced the pain away, succumbing to the dream. The dream was bad, but the reality of it all was worse.

"I didn't do it. I didn't sleep with him," I cried out as they continued to pelt me with hurtful words. I was dying without him.

"You did, you little fucking whore." I shook my head, wanting the hurt to go away. If only you *could've taken me with you, Diesel.*

"Look at me." A hand wrapped around my throat and my eyes drifted open. My focus was off as I was in and out.

"Let go of me." I spat out the words at him as I tried to wrench myself out of his touch. I was on the ground and he was above me, his movements off as my eyes adjusted to the lighting.

A smile crept onto his face. I wondered why I had ever taken that job at PGI. Was it worth it now? To me, no.

"You're just as beautiful as you were before..." A finger skimmed down the side of my face, and I almost turned my head to bite it off. I wanted to hurt him. To gouge his beady fucking eyes out. He deserved whatever pain I could give him, but instead of biting, I sneered at him.

"And you're just as revolting as I remember." I glared at him, praying that God would slam his fist down on him taking his miserable life. His hand slipped from my throat to my chin where he gripped it painfully hard. I could feel the tears welling behind my eyes but forced them down. I wouldn't cry for this fool. It's what he wanted. To break me, to hurt me. As If I hadn't been hurt enough.

"I think you have forgotten who you're talking to, forgotten who it is that controls you, who allows you to live when you shouldn't even be breathing right now." I numbed myself to the pain, crawling back into my mind.

"I miss you. I miss you so fucking much, and

you don't even understand it. You told me you would protect me. That you would be here for me, and I don't feel it. I don't see you. All I feel is the darkness descending on me. Breaking me."

"Listen to me." Roger's voice entered my mind, but I forced it away. I could feel his fingers digging into my skin.

"God, just take me. Take me to him. Let me see him again. Feel him." I screamed the words as I beat against his headstone. He had no idea what he left me with.

"If you won't give me what I want, I will just take it," Roger screamed into my ear. His voice wasn't a scream in my mind though; it was just a mere whisper. I forced myself from the present and into the past. Into the deepness... never wanting to come out.

"Open those creamy thighs for me."

"I hate you. I hate what you're doing to me. I hate that you left me when I needed you most. I hate that I miss your touch, your voice, your scent, and the way you made me feel like everything was okay. Why did you leave? Why?" I pleaded. My knees scraped across the stone. The pain wasn't even registering in my mind because the real pain was in my chest. Eating away at me.

"Fucking you will be exactly as I thought it would be." His voice repulsed me as he gripped my thighs. Why wasn't I fighting him? Why didn't I care enough to stop this?

"Why? Why?" I cried out over and over again. Find strength. Something echoed within me. Find

strength. The word played over and over again.

"Are you wet for me?" he asked me, but I never answered. I wouldn't. There was no hope. I had lost Diesel once again, and now I was going to lose what made me who I was.

"Fight him. Find it in you to fight him." The voice shadowed everything else. *It sounded like Diesel's, but how could that be? He wasn't here. My fingers ran over the engraved words, but I felt nothing. Air. I was going insane.*

"I'm going to hurt you, Maggie. Rip you to pieces and treat you like the little whore that you are. If you loved that monster, then you can love me, too." I could feel his fingers at my entrance. I wanted him to go away. I wanted it all to go away.

"Let go of her." I knew that voice. Shocked out of my stupor, I turned to see my dad in the doorway of the room. *How had he gotten in here?*

"Or what, old man? You going to kill me?" Roger said unfazed by my father's presence. I sat up pushing Roger's hands away the best I could.

"No. I won't kill you. There are a long line of people in this place who want a piece of you first, and I refuse to not give them the chance." My father's eyes burned into my face. I could tell he was scared, out of place. I was confused, and more than anything, hurting.

Don't let him win. The voice was back.

"Then what the fuck is it you want, Richard, as you can see I'm busy with your daughter." His eyes roamed up and down my body, probably finishing what my father had interrupted in his mind. How I had allowed his hand to stay in place on my leg I didn't know. All I knew was when his attention turned back to my father, I then grabbed his hand and twisted it until I heard an audible crack.

He pulled away from me, his eyes wide, as pain construed his features. He reached for me with his other hand, and I slammed my palm into his shoulder shoving him out of the way.

"Never. Touch. Me. Again," I screamed. I felt like I was going crazy, my mind gone. I was a monster on a path of destruction. I saw the syringe in my father's hand, and I knew what I had to do. Roger scurried across the floor away from me as I ran across the room and grabbed the syringe from my father. I had a mission to fulfill—a reason to live.

"I don't want you to feel guilty about doing this, Maggie." My father tried to reach me, but it was useless. I ignored him and uncapped the end of the syringe where the needle was.

"What's in this, Dad?" I sneered. What was happening to me?

"L1." Was all he said? L1, huh? I had been given that once before. It was a medication that knocked you out cold. Its side effects on those who weren't sick were useless. Or so I had heard. That wouldn't stop me from stabbing it into Roger's arm. I crossed the room in ten steps and crouched down on my heels.

"You'll regret fucking with me, Maggie. There are secrets that you will never understand and you will never hear if you do this. If you let them take me, you will never know." I hesitated for a moment wondering what it was he could know that I didn't. He was bluffing. He had to be. If whatever it was he thought I needed to know was so important, he would've told me instead of trying to rape me.

"I don't believe you," I hissed, stabbing him in the arm with the needle. I pushed at the end of the syringe injecting him with the L1. When he woke up next, he would be imprisoned, or better yet, beaten for all those he had hurt.

"You don't understand, Maggie. You and Diesel are connected." I stood, walking away from him. I didn't want to hear his lies, his manipulation.

"I don't believe you," I screamed again. Then I turned to my father and saw the panic on his face. Why was he panicked?

"What is it?" I asked.

"He knows the truth, and he won't tell you. Tell her, Richard. Tell her!!" He was yelling, and my head was on the verge of exploding. Too many voices, too much noise. I couldn't think straight.

"There is nothing to tell her, Roger. Nothing at all." The way my father spoke caused shivers to run down my spine. I could feel my heart beating out of my chest.

"There is. Tell her because if you don't, then I will." Roger's voice was going in and out in my mind. The look on my father's face said all I needed to know. There was more than I knew. More than I was being let on to know.

"Is Roger right?" I didn't want to question anyone else because I knew just how manipulative

Roger could be. But I also knew something wasn't right. I could feel it deep inside my bones.

"Tell her why you took the job working for my father, Richard. Tell her what she is." Roger's voice was fading. I clenched my fists together knowing what I was about to hear was going to change my life forever.

"What's he talking about, and don't you dare fucking lie to me. I can tell you know something. Just tell me." I almost allowed myself to beg, to be weak. Never again would I do that. I wouldn't lose sight of hope in this place.

"Can we just talk about this after we go back and get Killer out? He should be waking up soon." My father dismissed my anger and uncertainty. It was uncanny to say the least. I glanced over at Roger, who was now fast asleep.

"What are you lying to me about?" I growled, taking steps toward him until I was gripping him by the arm.

"I cannot tell you here. You wouldn't understand." He defended himself, shrugging away my grip before walking out of the room and down the hall. My gaze drifted from Roger to my father... What was he lying about? Without hesitation, I entered the hallway. The walls were white and clean. Making me feel like a speck of dirt. The tiles reflected my facial features from them as we made our way down the hallway. I cringed, tear streaks marring my cheeks at seeing the red marks from Roger's hands.

My father placed a key card into a slot in a

PROJECT: k i l l e r

door, and it opened. A glass wall and steel door separated me from Killer. I remember the way he looked at me, the things he said to me not that long ago.

He was lying on the ground in the middle of his cell. I couldn't even tell if his chest was moving. Fear seized me. If he were truly dead, I wasn't sure I could live with myself.

I pounded on the glass before yelling at my father.

"What did you do to him?"

"He was going to kill me. I had to do something, Maggie." A shiver rippled through me as I whirled on him.

"What did you give him, the same thing you gave Roger? What are you hiding? Are you even on our side?" The questions kept coming. I was so confused, afraid, and unsure. I was about to have a breakdown.

"Breathe. He'll be okay once we get him out." I clenched my fists staring at him through the glass. His dark hair shielded his face, hiding his eyes from me.

I hoped he was right because if Killer were anyone but himself, we wouldn't be able to escape this place, and we most certainly would be dead.

P a g e | **194**

nineteen

KILLER

SOMETHING IN MY head pounded. It echoed deeply through my mind. My eyes felt heavy, my body unable to move effectively... Anger bubbled to the surface, the past and present clashing as one.

More pounding. Where was it coming from? I forced one eyelid open, and then the other, gazing around the cell I was in. Richard was gone. Maggie was gone. I was alone. They left me here. For some reason, the thought made my chest fill with sorrow.

I sat up, facing the glass barrier. What my eyes landed on had me thinking I had seen a ghost.

Maggie. She stood there helplessly afraid. There was tension built up in her body, and she looked like she could explode at any point in time.

She used you. She wanted you here.

The beast inside of me reminded me of what

she had done. A growl rumbled deep within my chest.

"We will release you only if you promise not to kill us." Richards's voice came over the intercom in my cell. I wanted to laugh at his comment. It was amusing of him to ask me not to kill him as if they would indeed release me. If they were smart, they wouldn't step a foot inside of this cell.

"Well, that would be going back on my promise then. Plus, I plan to make your death far worse than hers." I sat up stumbling to my feet.

I watched Maggie's hand cover her mouth, fear riddled out of her. I could smell it—taste it. It was delicious, and I couldn't wait to sink my teeth into it.

"It was all a lie. A big huge lie, Killer. You have to believe me. You have to," she cried out to me from the other side of the glass.

She's lying. Something inside me told me that she could be telling the truth, but I refused to let my guard down. They wouldn't get the best of me this time, not ever again.

"Trusting you got me in here. I'm hardly that dumb, little one," I replied keenly. I watched her eyes light up with determination. Fear was pushed to the back burner as rage surfaced in its place. My cock got hard as she stared at me with anger in her eyes.

"Trusting me brought us back together. I know that you're inside there, Diesel. I know you know that I didn't do anything wrong." Her voice was natural, almost familiar.

j.l. beck

"STOP!!" I growled, my head feeling as if it was going to burst. I gripped my hair. Diesel. Diesel wasn't here. He no longer existed. Diesel was no one.

"I know you're in there. I can feel you in my heart. We did this together. We have come this far. Don't give up on me—on us. Please..." I could see tears falling from her eyes. Those tears meant something to me, or at least they should have. Her life meant something to me—I just couldn't pinpoint it.

Don't listen to her. She's no better than the rest of them.

"Diesel!" she screamed. That name. I would make her pay for trying to make me be someone I never was. A look of indecision crossed her face, and then she slammed her father's hand down onto the pad in front of him. The glass barrier that separated us opened, followed by the steel door to the cell that held me. Before her father could close them both, she ran through them. Straight to me.

The beast inside of me growled in approval. She was mine at last to do whatever I pleased.

"I know you're in there. I can feel it—come back to me." She reached out for me. I recoiled, my mind uncertain as to why I wasn't lashing out, why my hands weren't around her neck ending her pathetic life.

"Stay away from me," I screamed. The voice wasn't my own—the feelings coming to the surface were unknown to me.

"Come back to me," she cried out again taking

another step forward, failing to heed my warning. Within a blink, I was gripping her by the shoulders, pressing her against the nearest wall. My hold was gentle but firm, and I wasn't sure why. I should be hurting her... forcing her to feel my pain, making her bend to my will.

"Leave. Me. Alone." I pronounced every single word for her so she could understand. Nothing in her eyes said she was backing down, and that only made me angrier.

"Remember us, remember this." One of her hands cupped my face while the other forced my hand over her chest—her heart. I could feel the beat, the pulsing of blood as it pushed throughout her body. I tried to pull away, but she held my hand there, forcing me to feel her warmth, her beat. I listened to the rhythm, staring deeply into her eyes. She knew me, really knew me. I could feel it.

A snapping formed in my head, and I pulled away gripping at my scalp. Pain seared through my mind, and into my eyes. What was happening to me?

I fell to the ground, my knees bouncing on the hard floor. I could feel something ripping from inside of me. I could feel it pushing its way out. Like a snake weaving through the grass, it was going to make its appearance soon—striking at me while my defenses were down.

"What's wrong?" I heard Maggie's scream, and that was all it took to push me over the edge. Memories played out behind my closed lids. Colors of every spectrum were showing like a rainbow before me. Maggie.

Her delicate pink lips. Prom. A dress so beautiful it was startling. Her soft body beneath my own. Her panting for more.

A strangled sob ripped from my throat. My body was stiff as I absorbed all that I could, my nails dug into the floor. Then peace. Absolute silence was all I could hear in my mind. When I looked up at Maggie, I knew I had found myself again.

"You're here..." She cried out with joy, smiling softly. She looked like she had been battered and bruised.

"Are you okay?" I asked. I wasn't sure what had happened to her. I felt disconnected from what was taking place as if a block had been placed in my mind. I prayed that it wasn't me who had touched her like this. If so, I didn't think I would ever be able to forgive myself.

She nodded her head, gripping my hand, pulling me toward the exit. "We have wasted enough time. We need to leave now." I looked up to see her father talking. I felt a tinge of anger toward him but wasn't sure why.

I stopped just outside the cell. "What happened to Roger?" They looked between one another before looking back at me.

"Maggie put him to sleep. We need to get out of here and contact your people before it's too late." I tilted my chin up at him in understanding before pushing through the door. If we were going to break out, then we needed to do it fast. I was the biggest and scariest of all of us, the corporation's prize possession. I could kill anyone who tried to stop our departing within a second.

Silence settled into all of us, the knowledge that we may not all make it out of here alive running through our minds. Maggie gripped my hand in hers, a silent promise that everything would be okay. I pushed into the stark white halls. There were cameras all over this building. They had to be watching us, waiting for the perfect moment to pounce.

Our footsteps were heavy and loud as we ran down the corridor coming to the end of the hall. I allowed Richard ahead of me to scan his keycard. As we slipped through the next door without a sound, I knew something was up. They were making it far too easy for us. No way would they just allow us to walk out of here. At least not without being in a casket. Something wasn't right.

"We need to head toward the second level and then we can take the stairs," Richard whispered as if it would indeed hide his discretions. He had already turned his back on the company the moment he allowed me out of that cell. Richard guided us up the stairs, our feet pounding against the flooring loudly. Fear was eating away at me. Where were they and why were they not trying to take us out by now?

We rounded the corner and my eyes landed on the elevators. My gaze drifted to the camera in the far corner of the hall as we waited for the elevator. Time seemed to stand still as the doors drifted

j.l. beck

open, allowing us inside.

Coolness encompassed me as the rush of relief flooded me. We were so close to getting out, so close.

Those emotions were short lived as the elevator screeched to a halt, a screaming siren sounding off in the distance. The noise reached us, and I watched Maggie's heart plummet. We hadn't made it this far and through all of this stuff to have been caught and placed back in those cells. I pushed at the roof of the elevator. There had to be a way out.

"This way." I gestured, slamming my fist through the light and through the roof of the elevator. The draft of cold air shifted around us entering the elevator cart as I looked at Maggie.

"You first," I said, waiting for her foot to boost her up. She looked at me with apprehension as if I was going to turn on her at any second.

"Do you trust me? I just want to protect you... If you want to live, then we need to leave." I stared at her intently as she nodded her head yes.

Within a second, she was placing her foot in my hand so I could boost her up. I watched as her hands gripped the sides of the open space and pulled her body forward. Once she was all the way in, I could hear her getting to her feet as she stepped on the metal of the shaft.

"Hurry, I hear someone coming," I heard her whisper. I looked to Richard next.

"Go on, you can pull me up," he ordered me. Something inside of me said to push him up into the shaft first, but I listened to him, knowing he could very well already have a plan in place. I wouldn't lie and say that getting Maggie out of here wasn't my first priority because it was. She had endured enough of this place. So, I listened to him and pushed up through the small space, just barely making it. Shoving off the side of the opening, I jumped off to the side landing on my feet like a cat.

"Come on." I extended my hand down to him. Voices could be heard above us, and I could smell the anxiety rolling off Maggie in waves and each one that hit me grew larger and larger. The elevator started vibrating, coming to life, the lights turning off and on, and then it was moving upwards. I gripped Maggie into my side holding us both as I looked down at Richard.

I could tell by the look on his face, he wasn't going. "Here, take this. Get to the second floor and use this for the doors. Once outside, run," he ordered. "And take care of her, please," he whispered.

"Dad... No..." Maggie cried out. The elevator stopped, and I could hear the doors being pried open. Remorse crossed his face.

"You're one of them, Maggie. You're one of the healed ones." I blinked, praying I hadn't just heard what he said. He had to be wrong. He had to be lying.

"Your lying, Dad." Maggie shook her head in disbelief.

I watched as his face fell, and the next moment, the doors behind him were opening. "Be strong, baby," he mouthed as the guards grabbed him.

I gripped Maggie tightly, not wanting her to get away. I could tell Richard wasn't going to make it but knew better than to say something right now. How was I to tell the woman I loved that this was the last time she would see her father.

"No, you can't let them take him." Maggie fought against my hold, her voice hysterical. I looked down at her, knowing there was nothing I could. With a tight grip, I held her to my chest as I grabbed the chain above us. I needed to get us out of here.

Channeling all my rage, anger, and pain, I pulled us up the chain. My body went into overdrive. I could feel Maggie's tension and feel her slipping from me in every sense. She was crumbling, falling inward upon herself.

"He's gone, they got him," I gritted out, moving faster up the wall. I could hear them moving below us. They would be swarming us at any time.

"Stop right there," someone ordered below us. I didn't bother to turn around. I had one mission, one thing that I needed to do and that was get us out of here in one piece.

"He has a gun." Maggie shuttered against my chest, gripping me like a lifeline.

"Stop or I'll shoot," the man below yelled. His voice bounced off the walls telling me he was growing closer with every passing second. That was my signal to push harder. I looked up, estimating if I could make it. The exit had to be another ten feet up. I could do it. I had to do it. There were no other options.

I heard the gun cocking, the pull of the trigger, and the wiz of the dart. I swayed to the left to move out of the way but was a fraction off, Maggie's weight causing me to have to readjust. I could feel the prick of the dart against my skin. I smiled smugly—as if that was going to stop me. They had to be dumb to think that one dart would take me down.

I allowed a loud roar to escape my lips letting them know that they had forced the beast inside of me out. My fist slammed into the shaft as I pulled us up the rest of the distance. Once at the entrance to the second floor, I threw Maggie over my shoulder and pried the doors open, all while hearing the roar of the elevator below us coming up.

Pushing Maggie inside, I sighed in relief the second our feet met the tiled floor. We weren't out of danger, but we were so close, I could taste it.

"Where do we go?" Maggie asked, fear in her voice. There was a red sign above us blinking the word *Exit*. I pointed to it and we took off down the hall. There were stairs to the right, commotion to the left, and the elevator less than ten feet away on the verge of opening.

"Go... Go... GO..." I gripped her hand slamming the door to the stairs open and all but dragging her behind me as I moved as fast as I could. Before we were halfway down the first flight of stairs, Maggie's legs were giving out. Not wanting her to slow us down anymore, I picked her up once again, throwing her over my shoulder as I moved even faster down the remaining steps of the stairs. Once we hit the first-floor landing, I spotted another exit sign hanging over a door. I felt my feet moving toward it of their own accord, and finally, we pushed through it as we were welcomed by fresh air and sunlight.

Spots formed before my eyes as my legs started to grow weak. The dart they shot me with was starting to take effect. Stomping sounded behind us, and I knew it was too early to give up. We had to keep moving.

"We are almost free," I called out to her, jogging from the building into a nearby bush. The place was surrounded by forest giving us one option. Turning around would send me back toward the building, and going straight would send me into the city where they expected me to go.

Maggie was weightless against my shoulder as I slipped her off for a moment, taking a second to breathe. I gripped her by the cheeks, bringing her face to my own.

"They got me with a dart. I have to get you somewhere safe before it takes me out." She nodded at me in reply, her face covered in a mask of sweat, and she looked as if she were ready to vomit. I understood what she was feeling all too well.

Wrapping an arm around my waist, she steadied me. We hobbled to what I assumed was the east, but I was unsure. The dart they had gotten me with was certainly taking effect. My eyes started to drift closed, my steps off kilter.

"Killer," she whispered into my ear. My eyes

drifted closed again, and then popped open right away. There was a plane close by. Maybe the brotherhood had finally found us. Happiness radiated through me from the idea of getting Maggie to safety and everything being okay.

"Where are you going?" Maggie asked. I was following the sound of the plane, not allowing the one chance at escape to get away from us.

"We need to run." I barely got the words out before I heard footsteps surrounding us. Energy filled the air like a dart leaving its chamber zipped through the air. My mind was disoriented, my movements sluggish, I could feel the prick as another dart of L1 pierced my skin. I turned around, pushing Maggie out of the way, ready to charge and attack whoever had followed us. Her body hit the ground hard, the breath pushing from her chest as I slammed my hand into her back.

"Surrender now, Killer." It was the dickhead from earlier. He was here, outside the facility with us. Did he really think I would just fall to my knees and surrender? Especially with Maggie here. She was my one reason to get out of this.

"Not going to happen. Why don't you surrender? Then I don't have to break every bone in your fucking body," I replied, full of anger.

But even as the rage coursed through me, I felt the double dose of the L1 surging through my bloodstream at a rapid pace. There was a dull ache forming in my body as I fought against the drugs to stay awake.

Must. Protect. Maggie.

I needed to do something and do something fast before the darkness pulled me under. I wouldn't risk being taken back to that place again or worse, something happening to Maggie.

It was then I decided if I snapped his neck within the next five seconds, we could still make it to safety. Then my eyes landed on Maggie. Though my vision was blurring and everything surrounding me was becoming one big haze, I noticed she had gotten to her feet and was making her way toward him. In her hands was a large branch big enough to be used as a weapon but small enough for her to pick up. Not wanting to bring any attention to her, I engaged the dickhead. With his focus solely on me, she was able to walk right behind him without him even realizing it.

"You decide yet? If you want to live or die? Because if you walk away right now, then you live and if not, then... I will show you why they call me Killer." Before I could get another word out, Maggie was raising the tree branch above her head and bringing it down at an angle, the branch hitting him right along the back of the neck.

Adoration filled my body with the courage Maggie had just shown. She had risked her life for me. I watched as his body hit the ground like a dead weight as Maggie continued to bring the tree branch down against his head. Blood splattered across her face and chest as she brought the branch down again and again. Pain, fear, and anger in every lash against the man's body, a loud crack filled the air as the man's head caved in. Yet, she refused to stop, her eyes filled with rage. There was eeriness in her eyes and the way her hands gripped the thick branch in her hands. Brain matter coated her just as the blood had, but she continued to strike him until her arms grew tired. I could see the tears in her eyes, the sadness filling her.

Guilt instantly seized me. I should have stopped her. I should have screamed her name and told her enough, but I didn't.

Why?

I didn't because it sparked something within me. Looking at her covered in a human's blood lit a fire inside of me. I wanted to fuck her, push my hard cock into her while she squeezed me with her tight cunt. But more than that, I wanted her to unleash that same beast on me. I wanted her fingernails digging into my skin until I bled. I wanted her teeth marks all over me as she broke my skin. I wanted her, hard and fast. Dirty, defiled and deflowered.

This woman, the one who had just killed someone, was connected to the killer inside of me, just as Maggie and Diesel were connected. This woman was mine. My beast.

"Maggie. Let's go." My voice was gruff as I watched her drop the branch beside his lifeless body. She looked up at me slowly, and I could see something in her eyes. I could see the animal inside of her fighting to get out. She had reminded me of myself before I found her. Caged, afraid, uncertain of what was going to occur.

It was growing dark so there was a chance we

could stay hidden until morning if we found a safe place as refuge through the night, but we needed to get going. Since they had already sent one man out, and he hadn't returned, the corporation had to have other men out on foot searching the woods for not only him, but us as well.

Silence settled between us, a deep understanding of one another radiating between us. She walked over to me, gripping my hand in her bloodstained one and nodded. I can only imagine what she was feeling. The kind of fury coursing through her, the need for blood, for revenge, the all-consuming rage.

I didn't get long to think on that though because, the next second, we were running through the woods. The air pushed against us, the coolness of the night air hitting my skin, caused a coldness to sweep through me.

Our feet beat against the wooded ground, large branches, and roots threatening to take us under as we ran. I could feel my body growing heavy, my eyes were closing, my legs unable to move another step. I was praying to God something would show up out of thin air. I scanned the wooded area, my eyes snagging on something red in the distance. I forced my eyes to open more, zoning in on what looked like a small cabin. It was hidden behind a mass of trees. A small piece of siding could be seen just barely. I gripped Maggie's hand harder as we grew closer to the cabin. My mind and body were on high alert. At this point, anything good could be a trap. After all, this cabin seemed to come out of nowhere.

"I don't know if we should go in there..." Maggie hesitated, fear written all over her face. I couldn't blame her for being scared. I didn't know if we would be able to fight off any more men. My body was about to give into the drugs, and she was about to be alone.

"Come on. I got you. Be strong." I encouraged her, as I pushed the foliage away with my hand finding the wooden door to open it. With one small push against the wood, we were inside.

Agony filled my veins. I had fought against the drugs for too long, and now they were attacking my body. I fell to the floor weakly, my hands gripping my head as the pounding inside of it caused my brain to swell. I wanted to scream, but couldn't. My throat was swelling, my mind escaping me.

"Killer..." I could hear Maggie scream. There wasn't anything I could do though. I was useless. I was gone.

twenty

MAGGIE

PANIC GRIPPED ME. Killer was lifeless on the floor, his body unmoving. No matter how many times I had screamed for him to come back to me, he didn't.

"I can't do this alone," I cried out, my fists beating against his chest. Had I killed that man for nothing? Pain formed within my body. That wasn't me. I wasn't a murderer. Shame and hate for myself replaced my fears. What had I done?

My body ached as I heaved against the floor, my knees cracking hard against the wood. I had never wanted to cry so much in my life. Everything was a lie. I was on the verge of losing Killer, and I had killed someone. I took their life from them. Forced air from their lungs. This wasn't me.

My gazed landed on my hands. Blood coated

them.

No. I didn't do it.

I rubbed my hands together trying to rid my skin of the man's blood. Fear consumed me as I scrubbed harder. I could feel the shell that protected me crumbling to the ground. Who was this person who did this?

Pain ripped through my hands, but I couldn't stop. I wanted the blood gone.

"Make it stop." My voice was weak as I cradled my head in my hands. I squeezed my eyes closed, tension filling my body.

What's wrong with me? I could feel something inside of me ripping. Something inside of me was clawing its way out, attempting to make itself known.

"STOP!!" I screamed, unable to hold the pain in anymore. My fingernails dug into my scalp wanting to rip the affliction from my body. My head began to throb, like a bolt of lightning something ram shacked its way through my skin. The blood, give me more. I need more.

"LEAVE ME ALONE, plea... please." I cried out as I threw myself backward trying to resist the urge. My body hit the wooden floor of the cabin before bowing upward in an excruciating jerk. I squeezed my eyes tight as I was thrown into an alternative world full of memories that I had no recollection of...

"She's sicker than we initially thought. They're saying the tumor is inoperable."

It can't be. Memories flickered through my

mind. Riding my bike for the first time. My first haircut, the first time my mother held me. Tears lingered within her eyes. Why was she crying?

"Margaret, do you want to do the surgery with the meds or do you just want her to die?" Was that my father's voice?

The pain had to be causing hallucinations. There was no way any of these things were true.

"You're different, Maggie. But with that difference will come the ability to do great things for others. You were made to do good. You're an angel. My angel." I could feel my mother's words in my hair, her breath upon my face.

"It's a lie." My voice echoed inside my head. My throat throbbed from my raw screams, my insides churned, and I could feel the vomit rising in my stomach.

"Hang on, my sweet Maggie. Hang on." I could feel the prick of a needle enter my skin.

It's not real. It's not real.

My nails dug into my skin as blood seeped from the wounds.

"Because she is sick, the L1 will fight off the cancer in her blood, but, as a result, it will also alter her cells. This is a special dose of L1 made specifically for her type of cancer. Once her body has accepted the medicine, the changes will begin. After Stage 3 of her change, we will wipe her memory of her ever being sick and being administered this drug... but, in return, we need something from you." I could hear the cold tone evident in his voice as he strapped me down to a

small hospital bed.

"Anything. Anything. Just make my baby better." My mother's voice shook with every word.

"When she hits adulthood, and her cells hit a certain percentage of development, you need to bring her back here. Maggie is the chosen one. She will remove any threats without a second thought. She will kill in order to protect. Without the proper training, she could be a danger to society, her friends and family, even herself."

"What does that make her? Is she ever going to be normal? Will she lead a normal life?" I could hear the panic rising in my mother's voice.

"It makes her a member of the project society. It makes her a killer. When the time comes, she will no longer be your child. She will be trained to be an outlaw, a scoundrel. Logged as experiment 0001 and known as Project: Rogue."

To be continued....
in PROJECT: Rogue
The Project Series – Book 2

ALSO COMING SOON
INJUSTICE
A Kingpin Love Affair – Book 4

Continue reading for a Sneak Peek of *Injustice*

SNEAK PEEK — INJUSTICE

PROLOGUE

THE FLOOR WAS cold beneath my hands. A blind fold covered my eyes, never allowing a sliver of light to break through. Oh, how I craved light, sun, warmth. I could hear someone next to me sobbing quietly. I had been just like her mere weeks ago. Now I was nothing but the shell of a person. Beaten, battered, and betrayed by my own family. Sold into the sex ring.

I knew what would come of me—nothing. I would be used for everything they could use me for, and then, when the time came, they would discard me like yesterday's trash.

"Tony says we need to move them the fuck out." A man's voice I knew all too well echoed through the room. I had no idea where we were, what was going on, or who it was that had me. I had been drugged, blindfolded, and forced to sit bound this entire time. I had come to terms with the life I would be given.

"All right, man. You take the left side, I'll take the right side." A shudder worked its way through my body. I wasn't ready to be touched. I never would be. Maybe they would consider me crazy and just kill me outright.

"Let's go, princess." There was a tug on my arm that forced me to stand. My muscles protested, and my body threatened to collapse to the floor. When was the last time I had eaten something? Drank water? I could feel my mind closing in on itself.

The hand on my arm tightened in warning. Pain was about to come. "I said to fucking move." Rancid breath encompassed my senses as I felt him right next to my ear. Forcing myself to stand and walk, I followed behind him as he tugged me along. I could hear others moving around and wondered how many of us there truly were? What were they going to do with us?

"Now, you're going to go through this door and be a good little girl. No kicking, punching, screaming, or trying to escape. Do you understand me?" His voice promised horrible things, and I knew if I tried to escape, I wouldn't like what would happen.

I nodded my head, unable to answer him because of the gag in my mouth. I could feel tears sliding down my face but felt no emotion. Was there a way to shut it off? To make all the hurt go away?

With a shove, I was pushed through a door, my feet catching on what I assumed to be the door jam. I stood there unmoving for no more than a second before I marched forward. I wasn't sure where I was, or what was happening. I felt as if I were floating through time, waiting for my moment to come.

"Over here, princess," one of them whispered. I hated that they called me princess—or anything for that matter. My steps flauntered, as I tried to figure out where the voice came from.

"Two men coming in from the right stairwell," one of the men whispered. I could barely hear him and suddenly wondered if this was some sick, twisted game, if someone else was going to come and take us.

"Get over here, princess." I could hear the aggravated anger in his voice. I stood there frozen in time as I heard a door being kicking in. I wondered where the man who had pushed me through the door had gone. Why wasn't he leading me to where I was supposed to go.

"You cannot let them find her, Xavier," someone said. I floundered around. Blackness was all that surrounded me. I could hear voices... My mind was moving a million miles a minute.

"Princess, get over here, or I'll be forced to put a bullet in your head." I swiveled around in the darkness, trying to figure out where they were. Unable to answer them, I could hear the barrel of the gun loading.

"She's valuable goods, X." A muffled cry sounded off in the distance. If I were being honest, I would say I wanted whomever it was coming to find me. Maybe those other people were the lesser of two evils.

"I got this, man. Boss will just have to deal with it." I heard the bullet before I felt it. Pain seared

P a g e | **219**

through my body as a burning radiated through my arm.

"You missed, fucker." A voice sounded in my mind but nothing mattered but the pain. My body fell to the floor limply. Was I going to die? After all I had fought for, was this going to be the end of it?

"FBI. Come out with your hands up." FBI? I wanted to scream out, to tell them I was here, but I couldn't. Between the pain in my arm and the gag in my mouth, I couldn't form words if I wanted to...

Feet shuffled across the floor. I was on the verge of passing out. The smell of iron filled the air. Was I going to die? Inside, I was screaming... begging and pleading for someone to save me.

"It's okay..." I heard someone against my ear say. In an instant, the gag was being untied and the bag removed from my face. Bright lights flooded my eyes, and then darkness took over.

I was safe. I was being taken somewhere. I would be okay. I had to be. Right?

Acknowledgments

To my family first and foremost. I love you for allowing me to do what I do every single day. I know that the life I live is hard, and it means so much to me that you support me.

To my beta readers, the bloggers who support me, and my fans. Thank you from the bottom of my heart. You all make me who I am. Remember that, please.

To Brie, my PA, bestie, and sometimes the person I hate... Thank you for believing in me, for listening to my rants, and for making sure I do my best.

To Meg, Killer is your baby. ;)

To Lee, you're one of my best international fans. Xoxoxo

Also by J.L. Beck

—Bittersweet Series—

Bittersweet Revenge
Bittersweet Love
Bittersweet Hate
Bittersweet Symphony
Bittersweet Trust

—Kingpin Series—

Indebted
Inevitable
Invincible

—Project Series—

Project: Killer

Find these books under J.L. Beck at major retailers.

And don't forget to leave a review on Goodreads and where you purchased your copy!

Coming Soon from J.L. Beck
and in no particular order . . .

Injustice (Kingpin Series #4)

Project: Rouge (Project Series #2)
Project: Revenge (Project Series #3)
Project: Savage (Project Series #4)

Bittersweet Reunion (Complete Set)

Dangerous Ties (Ties Series #1)
Severed Ties (Ties Series #2)

Tainted by Her (HEA-Standalone)

Worth The Chase (Worth It Series #1)
Worth The Chance (Worth It Series #2)

Breathe
Exhale (Companion novel to Breathe)

About J.L. Beck

J.L. BECK IS THE Best Selling Author of A Kingpin Love Affair Series and The Bittersweet Series. She plays mother and wife by day and writer extraordinaire by night. When she's not writing, reading, or doodling, you can find her watching The Vampire Diaries and The 100. She currently resides in the tiny town of Elroy in the state of Wisconsin with her husband of seven years and their three-year-old hellion.

STALK HER—YOU KNOW YOU WANT TO:

FACEBOOK: https://www.facebook.com/Jo.L.Beck?ref=hl
TWITTER: https://twitter.com/AuthorJLBeck
GOODREADS: https://www.goodreads.com/user/show/23673426-j-l-beck
SIGN UP FOR HER NEWSLETTER: http://eepurl.com/2aydr

20470338R00133

Made in the USA
Middletown, DE
28 May 2015